Eva sat me down. As a new song started, she untied her top, dropped it on the seat, and began to grind her hips in my direction. With each thrust, my head banged into the vinyl behind me.

"I told him, let the bitch have the name," Eva said. "Let the bitch have the show. Let the bitch have the entire city of brotherly love, for all I care. I got the hell out of town. Had to go into debt to make the move, but I get to New York, score some bookings, start rebuilding my rep, and everything's going pretty well…and then…" Eva's voice trailed off. She took a deep breath, and when she looked at me again there was a fire in her eyes that made me nervous. "Then she walks into that goddamn bar last night. I got out of her life, she could at least have the decency to stay out of mine. But no. She can't just let it go."

"And when you saw her walk in, you were ready to kill her?"

Eva dropped to the bench, straddling my lap. She pressed her chest against mine, and leaned in close. Her lips brushed my cheek, and I could feel her breath in my ear.

"Porky, honey, baby, sweetheart, be careful what you accuse me of, especially in here," she whispered. "You could be on the sidewalk and bleeding in five seconds. All I have to do is nod…"

The CORPSE Wore PASTIES

by Jonny Porkpie

A HARD CASE CRIME NOVEL

A HARD CASE CRIME BOOK

(HCC-062)

First Hard Case Crime edition: December 2009

Published by

Titan Books

A division of Titan Publishing Group Ltd

144 Southwark Street

London SE1 0UP

in collaboration with Winterfall LLC

Print Edition ISBN 978-0-85768-361-8
E-book ISBN 978-0-85768-797-5

Cover design by Cooley Design Lab
Design direction by Max Phillips
Typeset by Swordsmith Productions

The name "Hard Case Crime" and the Hard Case Crime logo are trademarks of Winterfall LLC. Hard Case Crime books are selected and edited by Charles Ardai.

Printed in the United States of America

Visit us on the web at www.HardCaseCrime.com

For Nasty, without whom I'd still have my clothes on.

And for Lolly, who wouldn't have read it,
but would have liked that I wrote it.

Dear Charles,

Well, here it is, as requested, in all its obscene glory: a complete and mostly accurate account of the events that led to the closing of a certain bar on Eleventh Street. I've played it as close to the truth as I can, but you know me; I might have thrown in some slight exaggerations, the odd embellishment or two, and several completely fabricated erotic scenes. I just couldn't resist.

In other words, it's all true except for the stuff I lied about.

Best regards,
Porkpie

CHAPTER I
WEDNESDAY NIGHT

The heel of the stiletto caught on the strap of the black lace bra she had dropped a few moments earlier. She kicked it out of the way without looking. It skittered across the stage.

She held the bottle next to her breasts, so the audience could see that the pasties covering her nipples matched the skull-and-crossbones on the label. Then she lifted it to her face, and licked the large yellow letters on the label that spelled out the word POISON. She tilted her hand. Bright green liquid flowed out of the bottle and down across her chest. Green dripped between her breasts, over her ribcage, around her navel, and soaked into the cloth of her panties.

She threw her head back, and lifted the bottle to her mouth. A strange look crossed her face as the liquid flowed past her lips. A trickle of green dripped out of the corner of her mouth, down her cheek, and along the sinews of her neck.

Cherries whispered something.

The woman on stage seemed to swallow, then suddenly stopped moving. Her eyes widened. She grabbed her throat, and spit the liquid all over the front row of the audience. The bottle fell from her hand, hit the stage with a dull thunk, and rolled in a lazy circle around her feet, liquid pooling in its wake.

Great. Forget paper towels, I was going to need a mop to clean up after this act.

She made a strangling sound, as if trying to scream, but instead started gagging.

I looked at Cherries Jubilee, standing next to me as I watched the act from the wings. She shook her head. "Not this part," she said. "At least, not exactly. She drinks from the bottle, but..." The sentence trailed off.

The woman on stage stuck out her tongue and scraped at it with her fingernails, her mouth stretched in a convincing grimace of terror. Judging it purely on the basis of the performance—and I can't tell you how much I hated to admit it, even to myself—this bit was actually quite good.

The music ended, but the number didn't end with it. She kept going, flailing about the stage, pounding her chest, reaching out to the audience with a pleading look in her eyes. She jammed a finger into her mouth, two fingers, three fingers, and gagged again. She smeared the green across her face. Then her body went stiff and she fell to the stage, landing with her face in the cup of the brassiere she had just removed for our entertainment.

Great finale.

The audience thought so too. They clapped, cheered, whistled, hooted and hollered. A couple people were actually standing up.

But she wasn't done. Throughout the ovation, she stayed where she had fallen on the stage.

Not completely immobile; every few seconds, she would toss in a death spasm, which would set the audience clapping again, even louder.

Finally, having milked the bit for all it was worth, she lay still. The applause died down. She stayed where she was.

It took us all a minute to realize that it wasn't part of the act.

By the time we did, she was dead.

Half an hour earlier, I was completely surrounded by naked women, wearing only my boxers and porkpie hat.

It's not as exciting as it sounds.

In the first place, I was at work—we'll get back to that in a minute—and second, there was a distinctly chilly atmosphere in the room. An atmosphere that had nothing to do with the air conditioning, mostly because the air conditioning (as usual) wasn't working. This was the sort of chill that comes from a cold shoulder, and even though I wasn't personally on the receiving end—

Oh, right. Me. I should probably introduce myself. I'm Jonny Porkpie, known to audiences as the Burlesque Mayor of New York City. It's not an elected position— I'm self-appointed—but I do take my duties very seriously. I try to spend as much time as possible pressing the flesh and polling the electorate—

Sorry about that. Habit. That sort of gag usually gets a laugh when I'm onstage, hosting a show. But you're probably hoping for a more literate tone in your lurid paperback novel, so I'll do my best to keep the double entendre to a minimum.

But I'm not making any promises.

See, I'm a burlesque performer. And when I say "burlesque performer," I'm not talking baggy-pants comedian. Some have called me a no-pants comedian, but that's not entirely accurate either. My acts tend toward the humorous, sure, but when push comes to shove, and bump comes to grind, I'm the same sort of burlesque performer that Sally Rand was, or Gypsy Rose Lee—though they had certain assets that I lack. And that particular pair of assets might, to an audience, be the ones more likely to inspire lust than laughter.

Still, bottom line, I get paid to take off my clothes.

And so do all the women who were in that room with me.

The room, if you want to get technical about it, was a dressing room—although since we were in the back of an East Village bar perhaps "dressing room" is a bit of an exaggeration. "Oversized supply closet with mirrors" might be closer to the mark. The reason we were all in the aforementioned state of undress is that we were getting ready for a show. A burlesque show. Dreamland Burlesque, to be specific, which—though not the show I usually front for—is one of my favorite places to perform. It's been running for years and so manages to be both professional and relaxed at the same time, which makes it an enjoyable night for performers and audiences alike. In general, burlesque in New York City is a pretty friendly enterprise—most everybody gets along with everybody else, most of the time. It's nothing like you hear about in the old days, with one dancer putting ground glass in another's face powder—but like anything else, there are better and worse shows to perform in, and Dreamland was one of the better ones. Which made the current chill all the more unusual.

But not exactly unexpected. Because I knew the reason for it. And that reason was, much to my chagrin, talking at me as I attempted to get dressed.

"I know the setlist is already done," said the reason, as she emptied half a can of spray-tan over her ass. "It's just that I have another gig after this, honey. So if you can move me earlier in the lineup?" The inflection made it resemble a question, but her tone of voice made it clear that she wasn't expecting any answer that wasn't affirmative.

I told her I would check with the other performers to see if anyone was willing to switch. Given the rancorous looks being thrown her way by the five other women in that dressing room, I wasn't optimistic, but I figured it was worth a try; anything to get her spray-tanned ass out of that venue more quickly.

The reason's stage name was Victoria Vice, and she was the rare performer that absolutely nobody liked, including me. And for good reason. But unlike everyone else in the room, I was obligated to talk to her. Because I was running the show. It wasn't my usual gig, as I've mentioned (that one's called Pinchbottom, you can look it up online, and that's the last shameless

plug for it I'll throw in), but Dreamland's producer
and regular host, LuLu LaRue, was out of town and
had asked me to handle things for her.

And when a beautiful woman asks you to *handle her
things*—

Right, right, sorry.

At any rate, this Wednesday's performance of the
Dreamland Burlesque had been entrusted to my tender
care, which meant I couldn't join the rest of the
dressing room in giving this woman the silent treat-
ment she so richly deserved.

I pulled up my pants and, in my most innocent of
innocent voices, asked her what number she was planning to do tonight. I used the innocent tone because
the question was more loaded than the maid-of-honor
in hour six of a bachelorette party. Because Victoria
Vice was a thief.

I'm not talking about the exciting, sexy type of thief,
the kind who dresses up in skintight black outfits and
goes running around on rooftops, sliding into bed-
rooms while people are sleeping, reaching into their
nightstands and... But I should stop before I write an
entirely different book. No, Victoria was a plagiarist,
which in our line of work is the worst kind of thief you
can be. Maybe it doesn't sound as bad as stealing, say,
a pair of Swarovski crystal-encrusted pasties, but to a
burlesque performer it's much worse. "She who steals
my purse steals trash," the performer getting dressed
next to us had said, paraphrasing Shakespeare, after
she had fallen victim to Victoria's creative larceny, "but
steal my burlesque numbers and I'm gonna cut a bitch."

Now, Cherries Jubilee was attempting to appear as if she were focused on avoiding a run in the nylon as she put on her stockings, but I could tell she had an ear cocked in our direction. No foot covering requires quite the level of attention Cherries was giving it.

Victoria replied: "It's a brand new act, actually. Everyone will love it." Which didn't tell me anything about it, of course. A nice dodge. I would have pressed further, but she didn't give me a chance. "Which way is the little girl's room, honey?" she asked.

Little girl's room. What was she, eight? But I gave her the directions: out the door into the main room, follow the curtain that hides the backstage area from the audience (more or less), when you hit a door, that's the bathroom.

"Oh, no! Really? Out *there?* That's kind of unprofessional, isn't it? The audience will see me if I go out there."

I plastered an unconvincing smile on my face, bit my tongue, and explained through clenched teeth that since the house wasn't open yet, there would be no audience to see her.

"Hmph. Well, just in case," she said, and reached into her gig bag. It was a standard black suitcase, a "drag bag"—you know, the kind with wheels on one end and a telescoping handle at the other, the sort that stewardesses use to drag around their street clothes and burlesque performers use to drag around their stewardess costumes. Since walking into the dressing room Victoria had been clutching it between her knees like a reluctant lover. She pulled out a cape of the most obnoxious purple—that's not fair, the purple was fine, it was the woman who was obnoxious—and threw it over her shoulders.

"Thanks *oodles*," she said and, dragging the suitcase behind her, headed for the door, where she ran into the show's tech guy, an 8os-throwback named DJ Casey, on his way in. Casey stepped aside to let her pass. Instead, she blocked the doorway and pointed a finger at him.

"You. What was your name again? Charlie?"

"Casey," said Casey.

"You handle the music for this show?" Victoria said.

"Um, yeah…I'm the DJ, yeah," Casey replied.

"Right," she said. "Look, play my music loud, okay? No matter how many times I tell you guys, you always play it too soft. Got that? Loud."

Casey nodded.

"Sorry, what?" Victoria said. "I didn't hear you. How did I just ask you to play my music?"

Casey looked puzzled, his standard defense mechanism when dealing with difficult people. He wasn't dumb, but he played dumb for special occasions.

"Um, loud?" he said.

"Louuuuud," Victoria repeated, making it a three syllable word. Then she pushed past him and out the door. Some of the tension left the dressing room with Victoria, but not much. After all, we all knew she was coming back.

"Wow," Casey said as he walked in. She must really have pissed him off—from Casey, that one word was the equivalent of an obscenity-filled diatribe by anyone else. He announced to the room that he was opening the doors to let the audience in, which meant the show would start in fifteen minutes. Then he pulled me aside and reminded me that I needed to gather the performers' music for him before that could happen. As he left the dressing room, he glanced toward the bathroom. His brow furrowed, briefly. Then he pushed the backstage curtain aside and walked down the aisle to open the house. As I swung the dressing room door shut, the first few audience members were making their way in and handing him their money.

I finished getting dressed (ruffled shirt, rigged with snaps for quick removal; bow tie; tuxedo jacket), grabbed the clipboard with the setlist on it, and took a deep breath. For the first time in my life, I wasn't looking forward to talking to a room full of naked women.

Cherries Jubilee is, in normal circumstances, a close friend of mine.

But when I walked up to her, she practically threw her CD in my face.

"What the hell is *that* one doing here?"

"I'm just running the show, Cherries, I didn't book it."

"Why the hell would you book her?"

"I didn't book her."

"I don't mean *you* you, Porkpie. I mean the royal 'you.' Why the hell would LuLu book her? Why the hell would *anyone* book her? Did you know she was going to be in the show? You would have told me if you knew she was going to be in the show, right?"

"I found out exactly three seconds before you did," I said, "when Casey stopped me on the way backstage and handed me the setlist. Speaking of which, do you want Casey to play your music right after I introduce you, or when you're in position on stage?"

"In position. If she the hell does my football number again tonight, I'll kill her. Hell, I'll kill her if she does your—"

"Didn't she tell you she wasn't going to do that number anymore?"

"Yeah. And I'm blonde, so I believe everything she the hell says."

I shook my head. "I don't think that even *she* would be stupid enough to do a number she stole in the same show as the person she stole it from."

"The hell you don't," Cherries said, and turned back to the mirror, checking her teeth for lipstick.

I didn't bother asking if she'd be willing to switch with Victoria in the lineup.

The next performer was putting on a corset, angrily. Which is no way to put on a corset. As I approached, she shoved the laces into my hand.

"Tighten," she said. I slipped the clipboard under my arm and pulled.

Jillian Knockers is a legend in the annals of bump and grind. First of all, she's not called "Knockers" for nothing. On the contrary, she's called "Knockers" for two things. But it's not just the obvious talents that make her a star; the woman has been in the burlesque business longer than almost anyone, and it shows. Not

physically—if you saw her onstage and tried to guess
her age, I guarantee you'd be wrong by a decade or
two, on the young side. Where it's obvious is in the
quality of her performance. She mostly does variations
on classic stuff like fan dances, glove peels, feather
boas, chair work. When she's on stage, she doesn't
make a single move that isn't calculated to get a rise
out of the audience, and she gets it, in every sense of
the word.

"*Tighter*," she said, as I pulled. "Hey, Jonny, I have
your opening line (*tighter*): Ladies and Gentlemen,
tonight Dreamland Burlesque is proud to present
(*tighter*) plagiarist Victoria Vice and a (*TIGHTER!*)
veritable Who's Who of performers (*Jesus, Porkpie,
don't be a wimp, pull harder, I'll tell you if it's too
tight*) the bitch has screwed over."

That was a terrible opening line. I wasn't going to
use that.

But I sympathized with the sentiment. Jillian, too,
had once had a run-in with Victoria. I'd never heard all
the gory details, but it had something to do with the
Gotham Academy of Ecdysiasts, the school of burlesque that Jillian had founded a few years back. (She
calls herself the "headmistress," a title inspired in part
by her side job as a dominatrix. Headmistress, I've
been bad. Take me to detention, Headmistress. Oh,
Headmistress.)

Jillian didn't like to talk about it, but from what
I'd gathered through the grapevine, she had a problem with a competing burlesque school Victoria had
opened in Philly. That was all I knew, except that

Jillian wasn't any fonder of Victoria than Cherries was.

"I can see why LuLu would want to get out of town for a show like this," Jillian said. "What I don't understand is why she would book it in the first place." She took the corset laces out of my hand and shoved her CD at me. I took it and moved on. Once again, I didn't ask about the switch, but this time for a good practical reason: Jillian was the final number in the show.

Angelina Blood just looked at me. Didn't say a word when I asked her for her music, just paused in the middle of applying a thick halo of black eyeliner. Her eyes had been fully surrounded by black when she arrived, and now she was adding more. She pushed a raven-black lock of her raven-black hair to the side, and her raven-black eyes (I didn't know if they were contacts, but I'd never seen her without them) flicked over to the banquette next to her, where a CD lay next to a pair of skull-and-crossbones-shaped pasties on top of her raven-black suitcase. She didn't say a word when I asked when she wanted her music to start, but those black eyes flicked to the CD again, and I saw that she had written instructions on it. She didn't say a word when I asked her if she wanted to switch places in the lineup with Victoria, because I didn't bother asking. I didn't feel like wasting my breath.

The last two performers had been talking together, softly, as I gathered the music from the other three. They shut up before I got close enough to hear anything. I decided I needed to make my culpability—or, rather, lack thereof—clear right off the bat.

"Just for the record," I said, "I don't know what problems you have with Victoria, but whatever they are I agree with you. And I didn't book this show. I'm just running it."

"I blame you *entirely*, Porky," said Eva Desire, an alabaster beauty with pink streaks in her hair. Eva had shimmied into town a few months ago. She and I weren't exactly friends yet, but we had done a few gigs together and got along pretty well—at least, until now. "But I'll let you make it up to me," she continued. She put on a breathy stage voice. *"Peel me."*

She handed me a pair of pasties, the small circles of adhesive-backed decoration that keep burlesque performers away from the long arm of the law. Due to an archaic cabaret restriction, although a woman can legally appear topless in the streets of New York City, if she wants to do so on a stage in the back room of an East Village drinking establishment, she is required to cover her nipples. Pasties come in all shapes, sizes and styles. This particular pair had tassels dangling from the center, tassels that would no doubt be twirled at some point during Eva's performance. I peeled the backing off one and handed it to her, careful not to get the fringe caught in the exposed tape. Eva took out a lighter and held the flame under the tape. (Professional secret—heat the tape, it sticks better.) She centered the pastie over her nipple and pressed it down, hard. I peeled the other pastie and handed it over.

"Okay, Porky, I forgive you," Eva said, bouncing to

make sure the tassels would twirl and the pasties were securely attached. They were. She grabbed my ass to let me know there were no hard feelings.

I returned the favor. I didn't want to be impolite. Eva squealed and I laughed and suddenly, for a moment, there was a bit of the usual good atmosphere in that dressing room.

It didn't last.

Victoria chose that moment to sweep back in, purple cape wrapped tightly around her, still dragging her gig bag. She parked herself in front of a mirror, straddled the bag again, and got to work finishing up her face.

In addition to snapping the rest of us right back into our bad mood, Victoria's entrance also reminded me that I still hadn't dealt with rearranging the setlist. Eva was the opening act, so she wasn't an option; I'd be damned if I was going to start the show with a plagiarist. Which meant there was really only one possibility left: Brioche à Tête, the woman with whom Eva had been talking. I wasn't entirely comfortable asking her, because Brioche…well, Brioche is *weird*, even by burlesque standards. And I'm saying this in an industry where people regularly glue inanimate objects to their naughty bits and make it sexy. Brioche's acts are unlike anything else in the business—they're more along the lines of performance art, though that's not exactly the right description either. Because when I say "performance art," you're probably thinking about that excruciating thing you had to sit through for five hours when your college roommate decided to "explore the world of live theatrical creation." This is as different from that as you can possibly imagine. Brioche's acts are compulsively watchable. You just can't ever be sure what exactly it is you're watching.

And in person she tends to make me a little nervous. Don't get me wrong, I like her, but she has a way of looking at you that can be disconcerting. I can't quite describe it. It was a cocking of her head similar to the way a dog might look at you when confused, if that dog were significantly more intelligent than you.

"Listen, Brioche," I said. "Would you be willing to switch spots in the lineup?"

"With whom?"

"With Victoria."

"Excuse me?" she said. There was that look, damn it.

I did my best not to stammer when I said, "She says she has another gig, wants to do her number earlier in the show." I dropped my voice, not out of concern for Victoria's feelings so much as to keep the backstage atmosphere from going from chilly to explosive. "Look, you wouldn't be doing *her* a favor, you'd be doing the rest of us a favor. The sooner she performs, the sooner she leaves, the sooner everybody starts having a good time."

"Perhaps she could leave right now." Brioche didn't lower her voice nearly as much as I had. I'm guessing she wanted to be overheard—she doesn't have a very strong internal censor, nor much patience for dealing with people she doesn't like. If Victoria caught the comment, she showed no sign of it. She was busy adjusting something underneath her cape.

"What are the chances of that?" I whispered.

Brioche stared at me. I kept my mouth shut.

"Fine," she said, following the word with a sigh that would make a dead man punch a duck. "I'll make the exchange."

"Beautiful," I said. I took Brioche's music, and Eva's, and headed back over to Victoria.

"You'll be on second, after Eva," I told her. She thanked me "so so *so* much" and handed me her own CD.

Just for the hell of it, I glanced at the disc to see if there was any clue on it about what number she was doing, but no such luck. A self-burned job, nothing written on it but her name.

I made the changes to the setlist and headed out into the main room. Casey intercepted me halfway to the DJ booth. I handed him the paperwork and the pile of CDs.

"Thanks," he said. "I'll introduce you as soon as I'm all set back in the booth, okay?"

I nodded. Casey headed up the aisle, and I went back into the dressing room, where I intended to polish off the remainder of my pre-show drink in one gulp. But before I could, I felt a hand on my shoulder. I turned to find it was Victoria's. "Thanks again for your help, honey," she said.

Honey, my ass. I'd bet gold against g-strings that she was only calling me 'honey' because she couldn't be bothered to remember my name. I shook the hand off my shoulder, put the whiskey in my face, and directed my feet towards the stage.

"Oh, there's one other little thing," she said, following me, a little too closely. "I'll need you to hand me a prop during my act."

"Fine," I said. I held out my hand. I'd do just about anything to get this damn show started and her act out of the way.

Victoria pouted, which she clearly thought was cute. It wasn't. It looked like her lower lip was trying to escape her face.

"It's at the bottom of my bag," she said. "I'll give it to you right before I go on, honey."

Well, that wasn't fishy at all, was it? This, in conjunction with the death grip she'd retained on her suitcase all night, added up to a sneaking suspicion that our little thief was up to something. But I didn't have time to figure out what. Because on the other side of the curtain, Casey was announcing me.

And then the applause began.

Showtime.

I walked onto the stage, doing my Standard Politician Wave. A wink. A non-threatening thumbs-up. I took the microphone from its stand. Pause. A far-too-sincere smile.

"Thank you. Thank you. I'd like to thank you, the voters, for your support, and welcome you to Dreamland Burlesque!" (Hold for applause. The name of the show always gets applause.) "Me? I'm Jonny Porkpie, the burlesque mayor of New York City. It's not an elected position…"

I scanned the crowd as I did my bit. It was a nice-sized audience, almost a full house. The front row was packed with Dreamland regulars; folks who came to see the show every week, rain or shine, and could be counted on for a vociferous response if they liked what they saw. Good. Performers feed off the energy of the audience, and this audience would provide plenty of—

Ah, crap.

Somehow, I knew he'd end up in the front row. Near the corner of the stage, putting him unpleasantly close to touching distance, was a creepy-looking guy in a shabby overcoat who had tried to push his way in with the performers before audience seating had officially begun.

There's always one.

Look, I don't want to discourage anyone from buying a ticket, but if you're going to be one of those men who sits alone, refuses to take off his outerwear even when the air conditioning is broken, wears dark glasses and leather gloves, doesn't brush his hair or beard, and keeps trying to catch a glimpse of the girls getting dressed backstage…if you're going to be one of those guys, maybe a downmarket West Side Highway strip club would be more to your tastes than a night of burlesque. Burlesque is a different monster altogether. It's more about wit than anything that rhymes with wit; more about cleverness than any other c-word. Burlesque is a matter of brains over boobs… which, I suppose, is the standard arrangement, but you get my point. One creep in the audience working a Show World 1977 vibe could potentially sour the room.

This particular creep was sitting calmly enough and

had his hands where I could see them, so maybe he was one of the harmless ones. Still and all, I'd keep an eye on him. And while I was at it, I'd keep the other one on that group of gigglers in the back. Probably the bachelorette party I'd noticed gathering in the bar before the show—ah, yes. The white veil and penis-nose glasses on the blonde with the fresh-from-the-salon curls by the door were a dead giveaway. That bunch could go one of two ways: either they'd have a lot of fun and bring a great energy to the audience, or (especially if this was a late stop on their drinking tour) they might forget that they were supposed to be spectators and not the stars of the show. At least they were in the back row.

No worries about the rest of the audience, though. Looked like it was mostly groups of friends having a night on the town, couples out for a romantic evening —the bread and butter of any successful night of burlesque. They were here to have fun, to laugh at the half-assed double entendre, to cheer and whistle. Perfect. With a good crowd like this, when the lights hit the glitter, the underwear hit the floor, and the hooting and hollering filled the room, backstage would be a distant memory.

I glanced into the wings, and a thumbs-up from Eva told me she was ready to go. So I wrapped up my opening bit. "My erstwhile predecessor, Mayor Fiorello La Guardia, called burlesque, just before he banned it from New York, 'entertainment for morons and per-verts.' So, my dear morons, gentle perverts…welcome to the show." That line always gets cheers, both from the morons and the perverts. The applause kept coming as I introduced Eva, and got louder when they saw her walk out onto the stage to start her number.

What can I say about Eva Desire's performance? Let me put it this way: When she moves, you follow every step. When she doesn't move, you hold your breath and wait. And when she looks out at the audience and smiles, every person watching is convinced that he or she is the one that Eva wants to go home with. Usually, the burlesque acts I love best are built around humor, plot, or character, and Eva doesn't go in for any of that, but in her case I don't give a damn.

Four minutes and a whole lot of sexy later, Eva's costume lay scattered across the stage, leaving only pasties and a g-string to keep her legal. She spun in place so every bit of glitter on her nearly naked body— and there was a lot of it—caught the lights, a sparkly whirlwind of va-va-voom, and then she fell into a split that would have broken a less flexible person in half. With her long legs splayed from one side of the stage to the other, she bounced, which made the tassels (the ones on those pasties I had peeled for her) twirl.

And twirl.

And twirl.

Her song ended.

The applause began.

And that, ladies and gents, is how you open a show. The textbook definition of "a hard act to follow."

I wasn't at all unhappy that Victoria Vice was the one who had to do it.

Eva rolled out of her split, took a coy little bow, and

headed offstage as I made my way on. As we passed each other, she grabbed my ass again. "Knock 'em dead, Porky," she whispered. "Especially *her*." She winked and inclined her head toward Victoria, who was waiting in the wings.

I winked back, grabbed the microphone, and said to the audience: "Miss Eva Desire, ladies and gentlemen! That's one to write home about…if you're into that sort of thing." I made a few more lascivious comments—several more, actually, than I usually would, trying to delay the moment when I had to announce Victoria. Introducing a performer you don't like is a highwire act. On the one hand, you owe it to your paying customers to give them a polished, professional show. So you can't really say anything *bad*. But it was difficult to work up any enthusiasm for our little plagiarist, and audiences can tell when you're lying. Fortunately, equivocation is far less detectible, and it always gets a chuckle from those in the know. So in these situations I'll usually say something like, "I'm sure you'll enjoy her performance *as much as I do*."

But this time, I felt I had to take it further, for Cherries' sake. And, hell, for my own. Just get one little dig in. So what I said was this: "Our next performer comes to us all the way from Philadelphia, where she's well known for doing some of the best acts in burlesque."

I heard a "Ha!" from the dressing room that sounded like Cherries. Yeah, she's known for doing some of the best acts in burlesque. None of them her own.

"And now…" I said.

Big pause.

"…Victoria Vice."

There was scattered applause from the people in the audience who didn't know any better. Too bad. If they were expecting another act of Eva's caliber, they were about to be sorely disappointed.

I stepped off the stage and passed Victoria in the wings. "Thanks for the intro," she said. I couldn't tell if she was being sarcastic. She pulled something out of her suitcase and pressed it into my hand.

Right. Her damn prop.

"Just give it to me when I reach for it," she said, and scampered past me. The way she'd been guarding it, I half expected her to drag that suitcase on stage with her, but no. She left it sitting in the wings next to me. Whatever she had been trying to protect was probably on stage with her right now.

Or in my hand.

I looked down.

The prop I was holding was, according to the yellow letters (and skull and crossbones) on the label, a bottle of poison.

On the bright side, that meant she wasn't doing Cherries' football number.

But was she stealing from another performer? Did I know anyone who did a number with a bottle of poison in it? Off the top of my head, I couldn't think of any. So maybe, just maybe, this was an original creation.

Which probably wasn't great news for the people who had to watch the act, but at least it meant the show would run more smoothly.

Victoria walked out to center stage and threw off the purple cape to reveal a gothic black ballgown. Her music began playing—louuuuud (actually, a bit too loud, probably Casey exacting a minor revenge for her behavior)—and she began to dance.

She wasn't the complete embarrassment I thought she might be, but…meh. Even if she hadn't been a plagiarist, Victoria just wasn't a great performer. I hoped she would take the prop off my hands soon, so I could stop wasting time watching her and get back to my whiskey.

As the music crescendoed, she reached under her dress, gasped (unconvincingly) as if with pleasure, and pulled a black rose from the folds of the fabric. She smelled the flower, caressed her cheek with it, licked it, growled at it, and bit all the petals off.

The bit was getting a pretty vocal reaction. Not from the audience, though. From behind me, in the dressing room. A perturbed mumbling, but that was to be expected. As long as they kept the volume low enough so the audience couldn't hear, the performers backstage could make whatever comments they wanted.

Victoria spit out the rose petals all over the first row of the audience, then unzipped her gown and let it drop to the floor. She kicked it to the side of the stage, danced towards me, and extended her arm.

She wanted her prop. Fine. I shoved the bottle into

her hand, glad to be rid of it, glad her act was almost over. I turned away, planning to spend the rest of Victoria's number talking to people who didn't turn my stomach. But what was happening in the dressing room stopped me in my tracks.

Through the open door I saw Angelina Blood standing, frozen, in the middle of the room, wearing a gothic ballgown, clutching a bottle of poison in one hand and a black rose in the other. Her raven-black eyes stared past me. From where she was standing she had a clear view of the stage. A clear view of what I now realized was Victoria Vice in the process of ripping off her act. The very act she was planning to do later in the show.

I'd been wrong earlier, and Cherries had been right. Victoria *was* stupid enough, or maybe just plain crazy enough, to do a stolen number in the same show as the person she stole it from.

I glanced back at the stage. Victoria was displaying the bottle to the audience—Pest-Aside Liquid Rat Poison, same as the one currently gripped in Angelina's shaking fist. You'd think she would at least change the brand. But no. Not Victoria. When she steals an act, she goes whole hog.

And, damn her, *that* was the reason she had asked to be moved earlier in the lineup—not because she had another gig, but because in the original order, she was scheduled to perform *after* Angelina. Victoria must have seen Angelina unpack her bag, seen the props in it, and known that Angelina was planning to do the same number she was planning to steal.

And Victoria wanted to do her stolen version first.

I just stood there, looking back and forth from the stage to the dressing room. I didn't know what else to do. Around Angelina, the room was a flurry of activity. Eva, naked except for her shoes, was trying to comfort her, with no success. Brioche was elbows-deep in her gig bag, pulling costume pieces out one by one and offering them to Angelina along with suggestions about how she might improvise a replacement number. Jillian was holding the setlist. "You don't have to go on," she said. "There's enough people in the show tonight, we can just skip your number."

Cherries, top half a football player, bottom half wearing only a thong, was pacing back and forth. When she saw me looking in at the door, she came over.

"Why in the hell would you hand her that bottle?" she said, poking me in the chest.

"Because I didn't know," I whispered. "Damn it, I've never seen Angelina do that number."

We looked at the stage. I considered walking out and stopping the act…but no. I couldn't, because of the audience. It wasn't their fault they'd paid to see a show with a thief in it. And whatever happens—if the lights go out, or your music doesn't play, or your props don't work, or your pants get stuck on your hat—you find a way keep it going. You find a way to make it seem like everything was part of the act. The show must go on. The clothes must come off.

Cherries knew it as well as I did. Everyone in that dressing room did. So we did the only thing we could do. We stood and watched.

"I don't believe it," Cherries whispered. "It's exactly the same. *Everything* that bitch is doing, exactly the same as Angelina's act."

This was the final straw. We'd let it go on too long. Victoria would need to be dealt with. If I knew anything about the women in that dressing room, she would be, the moment she stepped offstage. But I couldn't just let the audience sit there thinking they had seen an original creation. So I decided that when Victoria finished I would give her the outro of a lifetime. *Performing an act created by Angelina Blood, I would say, the consummate mimic, Victoria Vice! Thanks for the sneak preview, but don't worry, folks — you'll get to see the original and best version of that act a little later in the show.* That is, if Angelina decided to do it.

On stage, Victoria turned her back to the audience and took off her bra, tossing it to the side. From where we stood, Cherries and I could see that her pasties were in the shape of a skull and crossbones.

"Even the pasties," Cherries said.

Victoria pressed an arm pressed across her chest, concealing the pertinent bits. She turned to face the audience.

Cherries was muttering murderously. *And hey,* I would add, *if you want to see Victoria do more of other people's acts, she's also ripped off Cherries Jubilee!*

She took her arm away slowly, holding the skull-and-bones on the label next to the skull-and-bones on her nipples. She held up the bottle, licked it, and let a deadly looking green liquid flow from it over her collarbone. It ran down her breasts, covering one pastie at a time, turning the white skulls bright green.

Victoria tipped the bottle to increase the flow. The green dripped down across her ribs, over her belly, to her black lace panties. Still pouring, she brought the bottle up to her mouth, where it filled and overflowed those red lips, ran down her chin, and dripped onto the stage.

"And then she dies," Cherries whispered.

And then she did.

CHAPTER 2

"So this was what, exactly? That you were doin'? Some kinda strip show?" said Officer Brooklyn.

"Some kinda titty show?" echoed Officer Bronx.

The audition was going great. If I were looking for a parody of New York City cops to cast in a burlesque show, I couldn't do better than these two. One male, one female, both short, stocky yet muscular, and the accents were dead on. The set was perfect as well, if low-budget: a folding table and a couple of chairs in a dank room illuminated by a single fluorescent. Flickering, naturally. The only alteration I might make would be to the lighting: I'd prefer a naked electric bulb swinging slowly back and forth for the duration of the scene.

Unfortunately, this wasn't an audition, I wasn't the casting director, and the people in front of me weren't character actors. It wasn't a set, either. I was talking with two genuine officers of the genuine NYPD, and this was a genuine back room of the genuine Ninth Precinct, conveniently located just a few genuine blocks away from Topkapi. Which meant we didn't have far to go when the friendly policeman asked me, very nicely, if I'd like to take a little ride with him in his genuine squad car.

And so here we were.

°

"Burlesque show, actually," I answered. I was still wearing my tux, which offered an elegant and whimsical counterpoint to the gritty modern realism of my surroundings.

"Oh, yeah?" said Bronx. She attempted a bemused expression.

"And what kinda thing goes on in your, uh, 'burlesque' show?" said Brooklyn. Those weren't the officers' names, by the way. Those were their accents. The names were unmemorable, but the accents stuck with you.

I said, "Burlesque."

Brooklyn: "What's that, like comedy?"

Bronx: "Comedy, or something?"

Me: "Among other things, yes."

Since I seemed to be the only person the police had invited on this field trip to the precinct, I figured I was currently in a final round of auditions myself. For the role of main suspect. I had plenty of lines, which I usually like, but I wasn't all that thrilled about the direction the plot seemed to be taking.

Bronx: "Among what other things?"

Brooklyn: "Stripping?"

Me: "Dancing, performance art, that sort of thing."

Bronx: "Performance art, eh?"

Brooklyn: "Anybody ever, you know, take off their clothes during this 'performance art,' or what?"

Me: "Yes. You've got me. I confess: People performing in a burlesque show usually take off their clothes."

Brooklyn: "So, then, they strip."

Bronx: "Me, I'd call it stripping."

Brooklyn: "They take off their clothes, they're stripping."

Bronx: "Lemme go get my dictionary, look up stripping, see what it says."

This was shaping up to be a fine comedy routine, but I'd heard it all before. I decided to derail it by getting garrulous.

"You can call it stripping if you want," I said. "I don't have a problem with that, it's just not entirely accurate…"

The 'stripping vs. burlesque' conversation happens often enough that I, like most professional ecdysiasts, have a standard speech with which to respond. People assume that we don't want to be called "strippers" because we're artsy snobs who refuse to be associated with such a gauche occupation. That's just not the case. We're linguistic snobs who refuse to be associated with words used incorrectly. It's a matter of accuracy, not pretension. In fact, quite a few burlesque performers were (or are) in the stripping business as well. They'll be the first to tell you: stripping isn't burlesque, and burlesque isn't stripping. For one thing, I hear stripping is a lot more work.

"…you see, officers, stripping and burlesque are indeed both forms of performance in which one takes off one's clothes. But they're not the same thing, any more than writing, say, a police report and a lurid pulp novel are the same thing. Sure, they both involve the act of composing text on a page, but the final result—"

"Okay, okay," said Brooklyn.

"It's about intent, as well," I continued. "The audience for burlesque—"

"I said okay."

Bronx chimed in. "So you're running your little strip show," she said, "oh, I'm sorry, your *burlesque* show…"

"And you're in the show too, are you?" said Brooklyn. "As what, the emcee?"

"Often," I said. "But more frequently as a performer."

"Oh, yeah?" said Brooklyn.

"Oh, yeah?" echoed Bronx.

"So you, uh, strip, too?" Brooklyn chuckled.

"Any chance I get."

"Oh, I gotta go see me that show," said Bronx.

"Absolutely," I said. "I think you'd enjoy it." I wasn't lying—people who walk in skeptical usually leave with a smile on their face.

"Yeah, right. I'll put it in my diary," said Bronx.

"You make a lot of money doing that?" asked Brooklyn.

"It's a living," I said.

"And maybe there was someone there tonight who was getting in the way of you making your living?" said Brooklyn.

"Maybe a certain performer there tonight stole something from you? Something to do with your livelihood?" said Bronx.

"Like one of your acts, maybe?" said Brooklyn.

Ah.

This is where it got tricky.

The thing is, Cherries Jubilee wasn't the only one in the dressing room that night who'd had an act stolen by Victoria. A couple of years earlier, Victoria had also added to her repertoire a number that bore an uncanny resemblance to an award-winning act created by the famous Miss Filthy Lucre. The act is called "Miracle Grow" and in it Filthy plays gardener to a wilting sunflower. Nothing will perk the flower up—not water, not plant food—until Filthy starts shedding clothes to encourage it to bloom.

And I'm the wilting sunflower.

Or, rather, my arm is. The sunflower is a puppet, and I'm the puppeteer.

So, yeah, as far as motives went, I had one. A fact that someone at the Dreamland show must have shared with the police.

"Look," I said. "Not to speak ill of the dead, but nobody liked Victoria."

"But *you* had a special reason, right?" said Bronx.

"Lots of people had a special reason. She had a real talent for pissing people off. It was probably her only talent."

"But *you're* the only one who handed her a bottle of poison," Brooklyn observed.

"You can't deny that," Bronx added.

"I'm not trying to deny it," I said.

"Fifty people saw you do it."

"Handed it right over."

"Not just the audience. Your stripper friends saw it, too."

"*Everybody* saw you put that bottle in her hand."

"So why don't you save us all a lot of time and tell us why you did it."

I sighed and said: "She asked me to."

Officer Brooklyn's face lit up. "She asked you to kill her?"

"Assisted suicide is what you're saying?" Officer Bronx asked, in a transparently leading tone.

"No. Victoria asked me to hand her the bottle. I didn't know it would kill her."

"You didn't know it would kill her?"

"No."

"Why not?"

"Because I had no idea what was in it."

"No?"

"No idea at all?"

"Not a clue," I said.

"See, that's weird," observed Officer Brooklyn.

"I think it's weird," agreed Officer Bronx.

"I'll tell you why it's weird. It's weird because that bottle says what's in it," explained Officer Brooklyn.

"It says it right there on the side of the bottle," Officer Bronx elaborated.

"Rat Poison, it says, in big letters," clarified Officer Brooklyn.

"So you can maybe see why," concluded Officer Bronx, with a note of victory in her voice, "we're finding it hard to believe that you didn't know what was in it."

Officer Brooklyn scratched his nose triumphantly. I rubbed my eyes.

"Well, I didn't think it was real rat poison, did I?"

"It says it on the bottle!" said Officer Bronx.

"Someone hands you a bottle says 'rat poison' on it, what do you think is gonna be in there? Rainbows and lollipops?" said Officer Brooklyn.

"It was a prop," I said. "Sometimes a label says 'whiskey' but it's really iced tea." (Not in my acts, of course. All spirits imbibed during my performances are 100% genuine. But more sober types have been known to employ non-alcoholic alternatives.) "So, no, it never crossed my mind that it was real rat poison."

Officer Bronx shook her head.

"All right. Let's go back to when you got to that bar tonight."

"Tell us everything you did from the moment you first walked in," added Officer Brooklyn. He tapped a finger on the table. "Everything."

I got to Topkapi early because I was running the show—

Officer Brooklyn interrupted: "When do you usually get there?"

"When I perform? Half hour, forty minutes before showtime."

"Every week?"

"I'm not in the show every week. And even if I'm performing, I don't usually run it."

"Who does?"

"LuLu LaRue."

Officer Brooklyn snorted. "You strippers and your names," he observed.

"So why were you running the show tonight?" Officer Bronx said.

"If you want to know about that," I said. "I'll have to start further back."

"Hey, take your time," said Officer Brooklyn. "It's not like there's anyone else we gotta talk to tonight, is there?"

"Last I checked, he's the only one here," said Officer Bronx.

"It was about a month ago," I began.

Filthy Lucre and I were sitting at the bar enjoying a post-show drink when LuLu LaRue wrapped an arm around each of us.

"Can you guys do something for me?" LuLu said.

"Right here on the bar?" asked Filthy. "Both of us?"

"*For* me, sweet cheeks, not *to* me. Not tonight, anyway. I just found out I have to leave town next month for a couple days, and I need someone to cover Dreamland for me when I'm gone. I'll book it, make the setlist, publicize, and all that, just like I always do. All you'd have to do is host and make sure the night runs smoothly. Casey takes care of most of it, actually."

"When?" Filthy asked, taking her calendar out of her gig bag.

LuLu told her the date.

Filthy shook her head. "I'm booked at the Gilded Heel that night. But Jonny is available."

"Am I?" I said. "Are you breaking up with me?"

"Ha ha, Jonny," said LuLu. "Seriously, will you do it? I'd feel a lot better."

"Sure," I said. "Why not?"

❖

"So you're claiming," said Officer Brooklyn, "That LaRue asked you to run the show?"

"Yes," I said.

"You're sure *you* didn't ask *her*?"

"Why would I do that? I have my own shows to produce. I don't look for additional stress. It was a favor for a friend."

"Favor…for a…friend," echoed Officer Bronx, as she wrote the words in a little spiral-bound notebook.

"So you and this LaRue are pretty close, huh?"

"Close enough to do each other this kind of favor, sure," I said.

"Way things worked out, bet she won't be asking you again, though, huh?" Bronx said.

Brooklyn chuckled.

Hilarious. And it reminded me that I was going to have to call LuLu on her trip and break the news to her. I wasn't looking forward to that conversation.

"So, then, tonight." Brooklyn said, interrupting my train of thought. "You said you got there early. When, exactly?"

"I don't know *exactly*—it was after 8:30, I'm sure of that."

"What makes you so sure?"

"The comedy show had just started."

Bronx flipped through her notebook. "Comedy show is supposed to start at eight o'clock," she said.

"And that," I replied, "is how I know it was after 8:30…"

CHAPTER 3

I got to Topkapi early because I was running the show.

It wasn't a dive bar. Not quite. But it sure wasn't a Broadway theater. Still, Topkapi wasn't a bad place to do burlesque, and the Dreamland show was always a fun gig.

The venue is basically two big rooms. The one you walk into off Eleventh Street is designed for drinking. It's fairly standard for the neighborhood—a long wooden bar lined with stools along one wall, a banquette against another, and a few tables scattered about between. If you were there when no show was happening, you might never know that behind the black curtains at the back of the room was a pair of French doors. And that through those French doors was a rather spiffy little performance space.

When I got there, the first thing I did was make my way to the back of the room and duck behind those curtains. Between the fabric and the French doors is a small alcove in which performers can store their bags until the comedy show lets out and we can get into the dressing room. There were a couple suitcases there already, so I added mine to the pile and headed back out into the bar. I glanced around to see which of the performers had arrived before me, and saw Angelina Blood sitting in one of the darker corners. Which didn't surprise me because—

✿

Angelina Blood—Officer Brooklyn interrupted—she was the one doing the same act as the victim?

Probably be more accurate to say that the victim was doing the same act as her, I said.

Another friend of yours? Angelina?

I wouldn't call her a friend. I know her. Not well. But it—

—didn't surprise me that she was in one of the darker corners because that's the way Angelina likes it. Dark. And by dark, I mean the lighting conditions, the hue of her clothes, the tone of her acts, everything about her. She doesn't wear a lot of what you might call colors, and the numbers I've seen her do have all had something to do with the devil, dismemberment, or death. Don't get me wrong, they're some of the best devil, dismemberment, and death acts in the business. She's good at what she does, and I respect that, but she's not a person you'd invite to a tea party.

Plus, she seemed to be in the middle of an intimate conversation with a girl with a spiky blue mohawk and a leather jacket, so I decided I'd put off saying hello until later. There was no one else there I knew except the bartender, so I sat on a stool and ordered a whiskey.

A few sips into my drink, Cherries Jubliee showed up. She pushed open the front door with her ass because she was trying to talk on the phone, write in her calendar, hold a cup of coffee, and drag her suitcase all at the same time. Once inside, she attempted to wend her way through the rapidly growing crowd. An offi-cious looking brunette with a clipboard in hand got out of the way, pulling with her a blonde girl nervously clutching a bag from the sex toy shop a few blocks away, but others were less accommodating; a ratty guy in an overcoat who walked in after Cherries glanced around quickly before shoving past her and heading towards the back of the room. And when Cherries had said 'excuse me' for the third time to a pair of fashion-ably unshaven boys feigning disinterest in their sur-roundings, I took pity on her and decided to lend a hand. I pushed between the boys, grabbed her bag, and brought it through the curtains to stash it in the alcove with the others. When I emerged, Cherries was sitting on my stool, and Angelina and her friend with the blue mohawk were walking in her direction.

I joined them. The mohawk shook my hand and introduced herself as Krash, with a K. She had quite a grip. "So, dude, you're, like, hosting this show?" she asked.

"Sure am," I said, and she shoved a flier into my palm.

"My band," she said. "Playing tomorrow night. Gonna rock. You can plug us, right? I mean, on stage? To-night?"

I explained that we usually only announced events featuring performers in the show.

"No, no," Krash interrupted. "It's cool. My girl Angel's gonna be doing a cameo tomorrow." Angelina looked vaguely surprised by this news, but nodded her head, so I promised them I'd do my best to remember, and stuffed the flier in my pocket. Behind their backs, Cherries rolled her eyes and hung up her phone.

Then Jillian Knockers walked in. After stowing her suitcase, she joined us at the bar and immediately baited me back into an ongoing argument we'd been having about whether or not a burlesque act needs to have "an arc" to be successful. We had discovered some time ago that we were actually in complete agreement on the issue, but we kept the debate going both because we enjoyed pushing each other's buttons and because it was an amusing way to kill time before a show.

Eva arrived next. By way of greeting, she kissed us all on the lips—everyone except Angelina, who doesn't really invite that type of casual intimacy—before she dropped her stuff behind the curtain.

Brioche was the last of the performers in the show to arrive…at least, that's what I thought at the time. "Order me a Sauvignon blanc," she shouted out as she headed towards the alcove with her bag. It took me a couple minutes to get the bartender's attention, and when I rejoined the discussion, Jillian had convinced Eva and Cherries to take her side in the debate, which made it three on one. I liked those odds, mostly because they sounded so sexy, so I jumped back into the fray and was in the middle of a defense so impassioned it had set Cherries giggling, when the wine and Brioche arrived at the bar simultaneously. After hearing both sides of the argument summarized, she agreed with me, but did so in a typically unhelpful way, quoting some French philosopher I'd never heard mentioned outside my freshman theater history class. Eva threw her hands in the air, claimed there was only one place she would be able to compose an appropriate rebuttal, and stormed off towards the bathroom.

I remember that I was smiling, because I was starting to have a good feeling about the night. Some nights you just know are going to go well. LuLu had booked a great mix of excellent performers. This, I thought to myself, was going to be fun.

I couldn't have been more wrong, a fact that would become very apparent in less than a minute.

The doors to the back room opened and the audience for the comedy show filed out looking vaguely depressed. We gathered our belongings from the alcove and headed backstage. As I held the curtains open for the other performers, the guy in the overcoat who had pushed by Cherries earlier tried to follow them in, but I stepped in front of him and explained the situation: *The house isn't open yet. It will be another half an hour. Feel free to enjoy a drink at the bar.* I thanked him for coming and pulled the curtains closed in his face. Even then, I had a feeling this guy was probably going to end up in the front row. He was just that type.

I made my way down the aisle and towards the door to the dressing room, but stopped halfway there when DJ Casey called out for me.

"Mr. Mayor!"—Casey always calls me Mr. Mayor— "Your speech!" He came out from behind the DJ booth and handed me the setlist for the night, together with a note from LuLu. At least, it seemed to be from LuLu; the handwriting was hers. But it said something I didn't think LuLu LaRue would ever say: that there was an addition to the lineup of tonight's show, and that addition was Victoria Vice. *I know it shakes things up a bit,* LuLu had written, the understatement practically dripping off the page, *but I'm sure you can make it work.* I started to ask Casey if this was for real—LuLu had been known to pull the occasional prank—but was interrupted when Eva Desire threw open the French doors and stormed into the room. She was clearly pissed off. Casey and I cleared the aisle as Eva blew past us, yanking her bag behind without regard for her surroundings. Her suitcase rattled back and forth, the wheels never quite catching the floor at the same time, careening into the seats with such force that one teetered precariously. Eva stormed past the stage, through the open curtain, and into the dressing room. The chair swayed on two legs for a moment before crashing to the floor.

"You'll never guess who I just saw out there," I heard Eva say, her voice loud enough to carry into the house where Casey and I stood, and perhaps even out into the bar. Before anyone had a chance to guess, she blurted it out: "Victoria. Victoria Goddamn Vice is here to see the show. I wish I was kidding."

"Hold onto your acts, girls," Jillian said. "She's on a fishing expedition."

"Do we have to let her in?" Eva said.

Casey picked up the fallen chair. I headed back to

break the news that the situation was in fact much worse: Victoria wasn't here to see the show, she was here to perform in it.

The reaction was about what you might expect, a cacophony of obscenity that would make a lot full of construction workers blush. There wasn't much time to get used to the idea, either, because a few seconds later, Victoria herself burst through the French doors and strolled down the aisle and into the dressing room, dragging her little black suitcase behind her.

We all got undressed in silence, an experience I'd never had in a burlesque show dressing room before, and hoped never to have again. I had just dropped my pants when I felt a tap on my shoulder. I turned around to find Victoria with a copy of the setlist in one hand, a can of spray tan in the other, and an insincere smile on her face...

As I continued telling my story, I watched the cops' faces. If I was reading them correctly, my narrative didn't seem to be diminishing their suspicion of me one iota. And any doubt about that observation was erased with the next question they asked me.

"That bottle you handed her," Officer Brooklyn said, scratching his eyebrow casually. "Here's the thing about it: only two sets of fingerprints on it. One of them belonged to the victim. That second set...well, whose do you think they're going to turn out to be?"

Subtle, he wasn't.

"Mine," I guessed.

Both officers feigned surprise.

"Oh, yeah?"

"You seem pretty sure about that."

"Maybe there's something you want to tell us?"

"Tell us now, things'll go a lot easier for you."

"Okay, I'll tell you," I said, "Between your blatantly accusatory tone and the fact that I'm the only person you invited on this little field trip, I figured I was probably the only person other than Victoria that anyone saw touching that bottle."

"Oh, yeah, Sherlock? So what does that tell you?"

"It tells me that I'd have to be a complete idiot to attempt murder in that manner with fifty people watching."

Bronx shrugged. "You said it, I didn't."

Brooklyn said, "Maybe you're too clever for your own good, what about that?"

"Or maybe," I said, "just to propose an alternate theory that doesn't involve me in any way, Victoria simply put the wrong bottle in her bag when she packed for the show that night. A real one instead of the prop one. How does that grab you?"

Brooklyn's smile turned into a full-blown grin. He seemed to be under the impression that I was digging myself a deeper and deeper hole. It made me nervous.

"You know what's funny about that?" he said. "We sent—"

He stopped abruptly when the door to the interrogation room opened to reveal a man wearing a suit that probably cost him more than I make in a year. His hairpiece was one of the best I had ever seen, and unless you were looking very closely, you would never have noticed the facelift. He looked at me, nodded, then turned to the officers.

"Representing Mr. Porkpie. Is he being charged?" he said.

Officer Brooklyn shook his head.

"Come on," said the suit, grabbing my arm.

I stood up and smiled at the cops.

"Well," I said, "It's been nice—"

"Mr. Porkpie has nothing further," said the suit.

"Tell your *client*," said Officer Brooklyn, "that he shouldn't leave town."

"Noted," said the suit.

"Tell your *client*," said Officer Bronx, "that he might want to keep his plans open for the foreseeable future."

"I'm sorry?" said the suit. "Can you clarify that statement?"

Officer Bronx shrugged. "Like the next twenty-five years to life."

The suit opened the door and indicated that I should follow him.

I did, but stopped at the threshold.

"Officers," I said, "I'd—"

"Shut it," said the suit. He pulled me out of the room. Too bad. I had a great exit line.

I followed him in silence through the station house, picked up my belongings at the front desk, and headed out of the Ninth Precinct.

"Thanks," I said as we walked down the steps to the sidewalk. I held out my hand. "And nice to meet you. I'm Jonny Por—"

"Don't care," he said. "Never mention this to anyone." He ducked into a black car that was idling in the
street. It pulled away with a screech even before the
door closed.

"Weird," I said to myself as I watched the sedan dis-
appear down Fifth Street.

I wondered who—

"I did," said the redhead, stepping out of the shadows.

CHAPTER 4

I gave the redhead the once over. It was pretty clear why she was keeping to the shadows—you didn't want to be caught looking like she did standing outside a police station in the East Village at this time of night. She wasn't wearing a damn thing under that piece of clothing you would only call a dress if you were in a particularly generous mood. It barely covered a pair of petite and perfectly shaped breasts and hugged every curve of her body down to her improbably round ass, where it came to an abrupt stop just below the level of decency. Red lipstick sparkled in the streetlight. So did the glitter in her eye shadow.

"I'm afraid I'm low on cash tonight," I said, "but I'll gladly pay you Tuesday for a—"

"Oh, shut up," said Filthy Lucre, and kissed me.

Filthy Lucre: my partner, co-producer, co-victim of Victoria's larceny, roommate, and various other things too numerous to mention, including wife. As I'd already explained to the officers, she wasn't at the Dreamland show that night because of her other gig, but she was for damn sure the person whose number I had dialed first after being invited to the precinct.

When she took her tongue out of my mouth, I said: "You got my message."

"Yeah. Halfway through getting dressed. Can you tell?"

"Where did you get that lawyer? He didn't look cheap. Unlike you."

"Kiss my ass. He was free. Unlike me. He did it as a favor."

"Really?" I grinned. "What have you been doing with yourself that a guy like that owes you a favor? Other than wearing that outfit?"

"Not a favor to me. To Jillian. He's one of her… clients."

"Ah," I said. She said "clients" in a way that made it clear that she wasn't talking about the Gotham Academy of Ecdysiasts, but rather Jillian's other job.

"Right," Filthy said. "I left my bag at the Gilded Heel when I rushed over here to save your ass from jail. Let's go pick it up."

On the walk downtown, I tried LuLu LaRue's cell number. There was an excellent chance that someone had phoned her about the Dreamland debacle already, but since she'd entrusted the show to me, I felt I owed her the courtesy of the call.

It went straight to voicemail. "Hi, you've reached LuLu LaRue and the Dreamland Burlesque. Leave a message—"

It was the middle of the night. She was probably asleep.

I hesitated for a moment, deciding if this was the type of news I should leave in a voicemail, then said "Hey, Lu. Urgent. Call me back ASAP. Sooner," and hung up.

°

The F Train rattled as it took us towards Brooklyn. I was looking at the ads above the windows without really seeing them. When we'd stopped in to pick up Filthy's bag, the bartender at the Gilded Heel had put a generous bracer in my hand and one on the bar for backup, but an hour later they were wearing off, and all the events of the night were buzzing around in my head like the inevitable sex-shop-sponsored vibrator given away in every burlesque show's raffle.

I was distracted. It's not every day that I end up being the prime suspect in a murder investigation. And with the evidence as it stood, it seemed to me that even a mediocre DA could make an excellent case against me. Means, motive, opportunity, fingerprints on the murder weapon—I had 'em all. And even though there was an angle for every curve in the dressing room that night, the cops didn't seem all that interested in pursuing them. (The angles, that is. Not the curves.) For instance, Cherries had the same issue with Victoria as I did. Angelina, too—after all, it was her number Victoria had been in the process of stealing when she died. And based on that comment Jillian had made about the show being a Who's Who of performers Victoria had screwed over, I was guessing that Brioche and Eva also had some sort of bone to pick with the girl. As did Jillian, of course.

But the cops didn't appear to care about any of that. Their only focus appeared to be…me. Which meant things probably weren't looking so good for the Burlesque Mayor of New York City.

I mentioned this to Filthy. She expressed the opinion that the police, as a matter of course, were probably looking into every appropriate suspect.

"You weren't in that interrogation room," I said. "They seemed pretty convinced they had their man. I think maybe I'd better look into—"

"Oh, great," Filthy said. *"Jonny Porkpie investigates."*

"What?"

Filthy put on her noir-est film noir voice. *"I couldn't get the dame out of my head,"* she said. *"That thieving brunette with gams up to her ears and a rear bumper that could activate any man's turn signal. Sure, she was dead now, but who wasn't? Well, me, for one, and that's why I could spend all my time obsessing, instead of talking to the sizzling-hot redhead sitting next to me. She was dangerous, that redhead. If I didn't do what she said, I'd have to suffer another beat-down at her perfectly self-manicured hands. But the image of that naked-ass corpse lying on the stage was burned into my brain with the force of a thousand raging footlights—"*

Maybe I was obsessing, but at least I wasn't getting quite so prolix about it.

"Look," I started, but once Filthy gets going, she's a hard woman to rein in.

"I decided it was time to make my move," Filthy said. *"To take to the streets, to pound the pavement, to hit the bricks, to flap my gums, to yank my chain. Because the police, with all their training and years of experience, couldn't possibly do it as well as me, Jonny Porkpie, the burlesque detective of NYC, who never*

solved a mystery in his life. But if I can drop my drawers onstage, I can drop a dime on a murderer. So I grabbed my porkpie hat and pulled it down over my long, beautiful hair and oversized ears—"

"All right, enough," I said. That was going too far; my ears are quite a nice size, for my face. Though it's sometimes hard to tell, because they're frequently covered by my long, beautiful hair.

"I get it," I said. And she wasn't wrong.

But here's the thing: I was the one that killed Victoria. Not deliberately; I'm not saying that. I'm not that kind of guy, however much I disliked the woman. But I *was* the one who'd handed her that bottle and watched, along with an audience full of people, as she drank from it. And then watched, along with an audience full of people, as she died. However innocent I was in theory, I could hardly deny that in literal terms she had died by my hand, and that didn't sit right. Neither did the prospect of spending time in jail—or worse—for the crime while a killer walked free.

Which brought up the question: Who was that killer?

I was starting to think that under one of the sequined pasties worn backstage tonight beat a heart trimmed with black lace; that one of those perfectly coiffed wigs hid a devious criminal mind; that one of those beautiful, naked women—maybe even one of those beautiful, naked women I thought was my friend—had made me an accessory to murder.

And I don't particularly like being an accessory.

I don't go well with your outfit.

So I had no other choice. It was up to me to—

"*Murder, he stripped!*" Filthy said.

"Filthy—"

"Let's assume, for the sake of argument," she said, "that this was in fact homicide, and not just some freak accident. Let's also assume, for the moment, that you're not the killer, because I honestly don't think you've got it in you. If you go off and start trying to expose the murderer—and, given the list of suspects, I do mean *expose*—what do you suppose that murderer might do to you?"

"I don't—"

"*Murder* you, maybe? It's part of the job description, after all. Whereas the police, unlike you, are licensed to carry loaded firearms, and fully trained in the use thereof…"

"But if they're carrying those loaded firearms," I said, "as they attempt to gather more evidence against me, it doesn't help get me off the hook, does it? If I leave it to the police, there's an excellent chance I'll end up in prison."

"That's better than being dead. If you're dead, you don't get conjugal visits. At least, not from me. I'm not into necrophilia."

"What if I don't go to prison—what if I get the death penalty?"

"You can't. Not in New York State."

"Are you sure?"

Filthy sighed. "Please, Jonny. Just let the damn cops do their damn job, okay?"

"Sure," I lied.

CHAPTER 5
THURSDAY

So here's how I wound up running at top speed across the Brooklyn Bridge, half-naked, in the middle of the night, pursued by all five members of a heavy metal band.

A full moon sparkled off the East River, its light shimmering on the midnight tide.

But I didn't give a damn.

The bridge was floodlit in the dark, its stones sharp with shadows cast. Its gothic stanchions loomed dramatically ahead of me and above, pointed arches grey and bright against the clear black of the sky, supporting the cobweb of cables that in turn supports the bridge. But I didn't give a damn.

Behind me, the Woolworth Building, for two short decades two turns of a century ago the tallest building in the world, towered still over City Hall, a single white cloud framing its spire—

But you get the point. It was all eerily, quietly beautiful, and I just didn't give a damn.

When you're running across the Brooklyn Bridge, and you look down, the gaps in the wooden slats of the pedestrian walkway run together—for you film nerds, it works on the same principle as the zoetrope—and the boards fade away under your feet, until you seem to be running on air with nothing to prevent you from falling down, down, to the streets of lower Manhattan, or the East River, or the streets of downtown Brooklyn, whichever of those three happens to be hundreds of feet below you at the time.

If you have any fear of heights, the view as you run can be downright dizzying.

I hoped that some of the members of the heavy metal band chasing me were looking down.

I know what you're thinking: Where did I find a heavy metal band to chase me across the Brooklyn Bridge—the 1970s? No, the truth is, just like they say, metal lives. Wherever you can find five guys with long hair and a grudge against the world, you're going to find heavy metal. In most places, five is exactly the number of that kind of guy you're going to be able to find, but those five will inevitably gravitate towards each other and form a musical experience guaranteed to drive you out of any open mic night.

But hey, who am I to judge? I work in burlesque, the top entertainment ticket of 1939.

And this is New York, where the rules are slightly different. In New York, you can find far more than five of that (or any) particular type of guy, and they don't all conform to the cliché. In fact, one of the five guys chasing me right now didn't even have long hair. She wasn't even a guy. She was about 5'2" in boots, and sporting, of all things, a bright blue mohawk.

Of the five, she was the one I was most afraid of.

A sudden breeze came up off the water, blowing my porkpie off my head. I made a grab for it and missed.

The hat bounced back down the bridge, towards Manhattan, towards my pursuers.

I stopped. I turned around.

I like that hat.

"You *hated* her," I was saying to Cherries, several hours earlier.

I had decided to make Cherries my first visit that Thursday because I figured I needed the practice. She was, after all, my closest friend at the Dreamland show that night. If I was going to question everybody about the murder (and it seemed like that was exactly what I was going to do, despite Filthy's attempt to dissuade me), I might as well start with the person I was most comfortable talking to.

It wasn't going well.

"Oh, I get it," she said. "Cops suspect you of murder, and you want to share the joy with your bestest buddies. Classy, Porkpie. Trés classy."

"I'm just saying—" I said.

"Yes, I hated her," Cherries said. "You hated her. Everyone hated her. She was hateful."

"But you had a particular reason—"

"So did you. And what about Angelina, for crying out loud? Whose number was Victoria stealing when she bit it? Angelina isn't exactly, you know, well-hinged in the first place."

"I'm not accusing you of anything," I said, and sat down on Cherries' couch. Her apartment was…well, how shall I describe it? New York apartments, especially on the Upper East Side, are not designed with the active burlesque performer in mind, especially an active burlesque performer with the imagination of Cherries Jubilee. Where in a 600 square foot apartment does one store such things as a two-yard-tall replica of the Empire State Building or a wearable scale model of the Hindenburg? The answer is: everywhere. Two dozen different acts were dropped, dangled, or draped on every available surface, shelf, outcropping, and inch of floor in Cherries' apartment. I'm sure there was some grand organizing principle behind the piles of stuff that filled the living room, but it wasn't obvious to the casual observer. Her storage techniques were as innovative as her performances; for instance, the shoulder pads and helmet from her football number, when not in use, served as the antenna for her television.

"I'm just gathering information," I said. "As much as I can. Yes, fine, you're right, I didn't like her either. Which is why I know exactly how you feel. But come on, Cherries, you can't deny that you had even more reason to hate that woman than I did. When Filthy and I told you we'd seen her do your football number at that convention, what did you do?"

"I got pissed. But—"

"And when we told you that she'd won the 'Most Humorous' award at the convention for that number, what did you do?"

"I got even more pissed."

"And when we told you that we'd informed the organizers that the number had been plagiarized, and they said they couldn't do anything because the judges could only base their decision on what they'd seen and none of them had seen you do the act, what did you do?"

"I wrote her an email."

"Before that."

"Oh, I don't know."

"Yes you do. You lost it, is what you did. You lobbied the organizers to revoke the award, and when they refused you blew your freakin' top. You remember? That night in the bar? The night you got the email from them saying their decision wasn't going to change, and that if you kept harassing them about it they were going to take legal action against *you*?"

"I was pretty drunk that night. I don't really remember everything I said."

"You said you were going to strangle them all, starting with Victoria."

"Well, I didn't mean it *literally*, you jackass," yelled Cherries.

"I'm not sure there's such a thing as metaphorical strangulation."

"Well, I didn't strangle her. Or anyone else. Nobody got strangled. All I did was send Victoria an email telling her to stop doing my number. Which, as you know—and as I know you know because you mentioned it to me just last night—she agreed to do."

"And you're blonde, so you believe *everything* she says." I got a certain perverse pleasure from throwing her words back at her. "And actually, now that you mention it, it occurs to me that I have only your word that you sent her an e-mail and she agreed to stop."

"Oh, for— You want me to show you the damn email? I'll show you the damn email." She pulled her laptop from under a pile of papers and opened it. She logged into her email, scrolled down until she found the one she was looking for, and shoved the computer at me. "Here, look, there it is. Enjoy."

I read Cherries' original message, then Victoria's response. There was something strangely familiar about the reply. I thought I knew what it was. But it wouldn't hurt to check. I grabbed my phone.

Filthy picked up after one ring. "Where are you?" she said.

"I'm at Cherries' apartment."

"You'd better be having an affair with her, then. Because I swear, if you're quote detecting end of quotation…"

"Did you save the email Victoria sent you when you wrote telling her to stop doing our number?"

"Why?"

"Read it to me."

"Read it to you?"

"Please."

Filthy sighed. "Hold on." The sound of typing. "…here we go. 'Dear Filthy,' it says. 'Oh, no! I had no idea you *also* did a number like that! I was inspired by one of my favorite movies…but I guess the acts really do sound similar. Weird! Now that I know that you do a number like this, too—' "

Reading from the screen in front of me, I joined Filthy for the last line.

" '...I'll *totally* stop doing mine out of respect for *you*. xoxoxo, Victoria,' " we read together.

"Yep, that's what it says," Filthy confirmed. "Did you hack into my email? If so, why the hell did you make me read it to you?"

"Actually, I was reading from the email she sent Cherries when Cherries told her to stop doing the football number."

"You're kidding me," Filthy said.

"Nope. It's word for word the same. She plagiarized her own reply."

"I'm shocked. Shocked, I tell you," Filthy said. "So Victoria had a form letter she used when accused of stealing numbers. Now that you've uncovered this vital piece of information, you'll be coming home, yes?"

"Not just yet. First I need to—" but I stopped there, because Filthy had hung up. Cherries, who had been in the room for the whole conversation, was rereading the email over my shoulder.

"Unbelievable," she said.

"So. You ready to talk about last night?"

Cherries snorted, took the computer away from me, and closed it. "What can I possibly tell you that you don't already know? You and I were in spitting distance of each other every second from the moment I walked in until the moment the show started."

"Not every second. I was out by the stage, talking to Casey, when Eva ran into the dressing room to say that she'd seen Victoria out in the bar. You were in the dressing room."

"Okay, so we spent one tantalizing moment apart. So?"

"So I didn't see how the others reacted. Did anyone seem less surprised than everyone else?"

"You know, it's funny, I had my surprise-o-meter in my bag, but I didn't think to take it out just then. How stupid of me."

"Seriously."

"I don't know, Porkpie."

"Did anyone's reaction seem strange to you?"

"Brioche didn't immediately do an interpretive dance about her feelings. I guess that's pretty weird."

"I meant—"

"Some might find it bizarre that we didn't all rush out and kill her on the spot."

"What about Victoria's bag? Did you see anyone touch her bag at any point?"

"Porkpie, don't ask questions you already know the answers to. You saw her. She had that bag clutched between her legs the whole time—at least, until she went onstage and left it with you."

I didn't much like the direction that remark was heading. I decided to try a different tack.

"When was the last time you saw her? Before last night?"

"Other than our weekly coffee date, and oh, every so often we'd take a nice trip to the spa, or a girls' weekend up in the Catskills?"

"Seriously."

"I don't know. Not recently. Maybe a couple of months before she stole my number?" Cherries stood up. "Listen, Jonny," she said. "It was great hanging out, and chatting, and all. But I've got a couple other close friends who are coming over to accuse me of murder later today, and I'd really like to shower before they get here. So if you don't mind…?"

She opened the front door, and I made use of it. But I wasn't done with her quite yet. I knew Cherries pretty well, and the way she was hustling me out of the apartment gave me the sneaking suspicion that there were things she wasn't telling me.

"Hey, wait a minute." I put my foot in the way of the closing door, a trick I'd learned in the pages of countless detective novels.

Unfortunately, those books were from a bygone era of hard-boiled men and sturdier shoes.

I gritted my teeth through the pain and attempted a last question.

"You had no idea Victoria was in the show until she walked into the dressing room?"

"How could I possibly have known? Did you know?" Cherries' fingers drummed impatiently on the door.

"It's just interesting that you happened to be doing the number she stole from you on the night when she happened to be there. Now, if—hypothetically—you knew she was going to be there…why, knowing you as I do, I'd guess you'd have chosen that act just to prove a point."

"If, hypothetically, I knew she was going to be there? I'd have found someone else to take the gig for me so I didn't have to look at the thieving bitch, rest her soul."

"So was there a particular reason you decided to do the football number?"

"Yeah." Cherries pushed my foot out of the way with a gentle kick. "I felt like it," she said, and shut the door in my face.

I limped the five flights from her apartment down to the street.

The first interview hasn't gone quite as I had hoped. I was walking out with not much more information than I'd had when I walked in. The only thing Cherries had been able to definitively confirm was something I already knew: that once Victoria was backstage, there was no way anyone could have gotten into her suitcase to mess around with the prop bottle.

But now that I thought about it, there was one person who'd seen Victoria before that. The woman who was in the bathroom when the rest of us went backstage. The woman who had emerged from that bathroom just in time to see Victoria Vice walk in the front door of Topkapi: Eva Desire.

CHAPTER 6

As I walked away from Cherries' building, I scrolled through the address book on my phone—*Bambi, Brassy, Bunny, Cherries, Clams, Cookie, Creamy, Dirty, Filthy, Knockers, La Femme, Monkey, Precious, Peekaboo, Ruby, Tigger!, Tim* (and so forth and so on; as Officer Brooklyn observed, we are an industry of interesting names). But Desire wasn't amongst them, at least not on my phone. As I feared, Eva and I had never exchanged numbers.

But I knew someone who had it. A woman I had overheard, just a few days ago, booking Eva for a gig.

Which meant I was going to have to do something I really didn't want to do.

I was going to have to call home again.

"Are you having fun playing detective?" asked Filthy.

"I'm not playing detective," I said. "I'm just asking questions."

"If you're a good boy and come home, I'll buy you a magnifying glass and you can investigate the cats."

"I need to talk to Eva."

"Eva Desire?"

"Yes, Eva Desire."

"She's not here."

"I didn't think she was."

"She might be here."

"But she's not."

"No."

"Do you have her phone number?"

"Yes, but…ohhhh. Too bad."

"What?"

"She won't answer."

"Why not?"

"She's got a gig right now."

"In the afternoon? Who does a burlesque show in the afternoon?"

"Not a burlesque show. It's another job. One at which she is unable to answer her phone."

"Where does she work?"

"Why?"

"I need to talk to her, and I need to do it sooner rather than later. If I can't call her, I'll stop by her work—maybe she'll be able to squeeze in a few minutes to talk to me."

"Yeah, maybe she'll be able to squeeze you in," Filthy said. She sounded more amused than the statement seemed to warrant.

"Can you, Filthy, without additional commentary, please just tell me where Eva works?"

"If you go 'undercover' with her, I want pictures."

"Oh, for—where the hell does she work?"

Filthy told me.

I tried LuLu again on the walk across town. Even though she was due back tomorrow evening, I was hoping to talk to her before she returned, to prepare her for the onslaught that awaited. I got her voicemail again. "Seriously, Lu," I said, "I need to talk to you. Immediately. Call me. It's really, really important."

Dozens of blocks, several avenues, two beefy security guys, and a good portion of the contents of my wallet later, I found myself looking up at Eva Desire. The cost of the beer in my hand—part of the drink minimum required on entry, in addition to the cover charge, which accounted for the anemic state of my billfold—would have purchased me a liter of the cheap whiskey we keep at home. But never mind. It was the cost of doing business, or whatever it was I was doing. Because Eva's "other job" was in one of those institutions one could frequent if one preferred a little more raunch, a little less irony, and a lot more physical contact with one's nudity than one is offered at a burlesque show.

"Eva!" I said. Eva is one of the few people I know who uses the same name for every endeavor. She's Eva Desire on the burlesque stage, Eva Desire in the byline of her articles for *Lick* magazine, Eva Desire topless at the strip club, and Eva Desire in the credits of that film she made, which Filthy insisted we add to our DVD collection. It was a pretty good movie, actually. A little short on plot, but...

Eva winked at me, wrapped her legs around the pole with which she had been dancing, and bent over backwards until we were nose-to-nose and she was thighs-, ass-, and shoulderblade-to-pole. Her nose, unlike mine, was upside down. Which meant that it was in the same state as the rest of her.

"Fancy meeting you here, Porky. What's a nice girl like you doing in a place like this?" she said.

"Do you have a minute to talk?"

"Do I look like I have a minute to talk?" The guy across from me slid a twenty into Eva's thong. She winked at me.

"When do you get off work?" I asked.

"That's the sort of question, Porky, that could get you kicked out of a place like this. Seriously, though, I'm on until four A.M., and then I'm going home to sleep. If this is a chat that needs to happen before tomorrow afternoon, you're gonna have to buy a girl a dance."

"Okay," I said.

She grabbed the pole with one hand, slid her legs down until her ass touched the ground, and stood up. "It's a date, Porky," she said. "You'll be the first stop when I'm making my rounds."

She whirled around and put a stiletto heel on the shoulder of the guy across the way.

Twenty minutes (and another hit on my dwindling bankroll) later, Eva was leading me by the belt loop over to one of the vinyl benches that lined the wall of this fine establishment. She sat me down. As a new song started, she untied her top, dropped it on the seat, and began to grind her hips in my direction.

"Eva, you really don't have to do that."

"You paid for it, Porky."

"All I want to do is ask you some questions."

"The questions I'll answer for free. But you bought a dance. I'm not going to rip you off."

"Really—" I began, but Eva interrupted me. In the interests of propriety, I won't say exactly how she accomplished that.

(I know what you're thinking. *Propriety?* Don't get me wrong—I see friends, acquaintances, and co-workers naked all the time. There's nothing awkward about that. But it is with slightly less frequency that they dance with me as their only audience, and in a manner that brings their mostly naked bodies in frequent contact with my own, clothed though it may be. It created a situation that was slightly more—how shall I put this?—*friendly* than I was perhaps completely comfortable with. To avoid sharing that discomfort, I won't describe the rest of Eva's lap dance, and instead will report only the meat—sorry, the substance—of our conversation.)

"Just relax, Porky. It's okay, loosen those shoulders—this isn't torture. For that you'll have to talk to Jillian." I tried to relax. She wasn't making it easy. "So," she said, "to what do I owe the pleasure?"

"Victoria," I said.

"Ah." She dug her fingernails into my thigh, just for a moment. Then she got gentle again. I asked her what happened between the two of them. She lowered her voice so the people around us couldn't hear the anger in it, and as the lap dance continued, told me her whole sad story.

When Eva first moved to Philadelphia, Victoria was the one who took a chance and booked her sight-unseen. That gig led to bookings from other producers in the area. Victoria put Eva in a few more shows, too, and they became friendly. Eventually, when Eva had made a name for herself in town, a bar owner friend of hers asked if she'd like to run a weekly burlesque show at his place.

"Well," said Eva, "there were no weekly burlesque shows in Philly back then, just a few monthlies. But before I said yes, I made courtesy calls to all the local producers who'd booked me. I didn't want to step on any toes."

"Let me guess," I said. "Nobody had a problem with it except Victoria. "

"Exactly. *How could you betray me like this? How could you steal this gig out from under me?* I didn't want any trouble, and I did kinda feel I owed Victoria something for getting me into the local scene in the first place, so I was ready to call the whole thing off. But then Victoria proposed that I take the offer, but with her on board as a full partner. That sounded fine to me at the time, working with a more experienced producer and all. So I said yes."

"How soon before you regretted it?"

"Almost immediately. I had to do everything. I came up with the name of the show: 'The Grand Coquette.' I made the postcards, I wrote the press releases—but when the press called in response to one of those releases, guess who gave the interview? Victoria's idea of co-producing a show was to take half of the money and most of the credit but do none of the work. Claimed that lending her name, experience and talent to the show was contribution enough. I stuck it out for a few months, but then—well, people didn't talk about it a lot around me, because they knew I was doing a show with her, but eventually I started hearing the rumblings on the grapevine…"

"About the stolen numbers?"

"Exactly. And then I heard that some of those rumblings included me in the mix. That was the last straw. I'm not working with a plagiarist who's going to drag my name down with hers. I've been called a lot of things, Porky, and most of them have been accurate, but I don't goddamn steal numbers and I never will. So I told her it was time to go our separate ways.

"Fine, she says—but since we started the Grand Coquette together, I can't use the name. Which is bullshit, of course, I came up with it all by myself, but you know what? Life's too short. So I change it. We're good, right? We'll just make it a clean break and stay out of each other's way. Nope. She actually calls the venue and tries to get them to cancel the show. When she discovers the owner is a friend of mine and isn't falling for her crap, Victoria goes around *telling* everyone it's been canceled. Posts it online and everything."

"And you have to start building an audience from scratch?"

"Pretty much. But she's not done yet. A few weeks later, a sign goes up in the window of a bar across the street. *Coming next month,* it says, *the return of Victoria Vice's 'Coquette La Grand!'* Coquette La Grand, Porky! Aside from everything else, it's illiterate in two different languages."

"No one ever said she was smart," I observed.

"I confronted her about it. You know what she said?

'I don't see why you're so upset. It's not the same name at all.' Now I had two choices: Either wallow in the mud and fight at her level, or let it go and keep my self-respect. So I let it go. Good riddance. I have better things to do. But *then*—

"Then the article comes out. Written by someone that I know for a fact Victoria is banging. It claims to be an article about burlesque in Philadelphia but really it's just a puff piece about her. And it includes a history of 'Coquette La Grand' in which Victoria takes complete credit for the months we produced the show together, claims she decided to move the show across the street because the first bar wasn't up to her standards, and refers to me as her 'stage manager' who's 'angry because I had to let the poor girl go.' "

"Wow," I said.

"My friend who owned the first bar offered to write a letter to the editor, but I said to hell with it." Eva had her hands on my shoulders and was grinding angrily, taking out her frustration and resentment on my lap. With each thrust, my head banged into the vinyl behind me. "I told him, let the bitch have the name," Eva said. "Let the bitch have the show. Let the bitch have the entire city of brotherly love, for all I care. I got the hell out of town. Had to go into debt to make the move—why else would I be working the Thursday afternoon shift at this craphole? But I get to New York, score some bookings, start rebuilding my rep, and everything's going pretty well…and then…" Eva's voice trailed off. She took a deep breath, and when she looked at me again there was a fire in her eyes that made me a little bit nervous. "Then she walks into that goddamn bar last night. I got out of her life, she could at least have the decency to stay out of mine. But no. She can't just let it go. She has to keep shoving it—In! My! Face!"

Eva, I had to assume, had some classical theater training—Shakespearean, most likely—that was informing her current performance. How else could one explain that she was (as Hamlet had suggested) suiting the action to her words, the words to her action?

"So you didn't know she was going to be in the show last night?" I asked, when I was able to.

Eva raised an eyebrow. "Please," she said.

"And when you saw her walk in, you were ready to kill her?"

Eva dropped to the bench, straddling my lap. She pressed her chest against mine, and leaned in close. Her lips brushed my cheek, and I could feel her breath in my ear.

"Porky, honey, baby, sweetheart, be careful what you accuse me of, especially in here," she whispered. "You could be on the sidewalk and bleeding in five seconds. All I have to do is nod at that security guy. Get me?"

"Gotcha."

"And anyway," she said as she slid back to resume the dance. "I'm the type of gal who wouldn't hurt a fly." The word 'fly,' of course, has several meanings. As a noun, in the context of the idiomatic expression she had just used, the insect was indicated. Her hands, however, were embracing another interpretation. Was she just doing it for appearances, in case the boss was watching, or was Eva deliberately trying to distract me?

"I wasn't accusing you," I said. "It's just that you're the only one who saw Victoria before she walked into the dressing room. If something happened in the bar before she came backstage, you're the only one who might have seen it."

"Sorry, Porky. I came out of the bathroom, saw Victoria walking in, grabbed my bag from the alcove and ran backstage to let everyone know she was there. It was less than a second."

"Why did you think that she was going to be in the audience, and not performing?"

"Because there's no way in hell anyone would actually book her. At least, that's what I thought at the time."

"Didn't the suitcase tip you off?"

"What do you mean?"

"Her bag. Her gig bag."

"What about it?"

"People don't usually bring a gig bag with them to *watch* a show."

"I don't think she had a bag."

"Say that again."

"When she walked in the door, I'm pretty sure she didn't have any bag with her."

"How sure is pretty sure?"

Eva shrugged.

"But you saw her walk into the dressing room with it, right?"

Eva shrugged again, then nodded. "Yeah, I guess so. Right, no, of course I did."

"So where did she get the bag from? If she—"

The song ended before I finished the question. Eva stood up and backed away. "Time's up. Sorry, Porky. Any more questions, you gotta buy another dance, baby."

I grabbed Eva's wrist. "Wait," I said.

"Porky, don't, they'll—"

"Was she looking for someone as she walked in? Did anyone in the bar—?"

"You need to—"

Whatever she was about to say, I didn't get to hear the rest of it. Something wrapped itself around my wrist and started squeezing. My hand was yanked off Eva's arm and twisted behind my back. I heard Eva protesting, but before she had time to explain anything to the bouncer I felt stale air whipping across my face as it rapidly approached the sidewalk.

I picked myself up and retrieved my porkpie from the street. The bouncer stood with his arms crossed at the door to the club. When I looked at him, he just looked back, but the message was clear. I touched the brim of my hat to let him know we were still friends, brushed myself off, and headed for the subway.

The collision with the pavement had knocked something loose in my brain. Or maybe into place. What I'd figured out was this: If Eva was telling the truth—and it seemed like she was—I now knew, or at least was pretty sure, that Victoria's gig bag had arrived at Top-kapi before she had. And, for that matter, before I had.

So had one of the performers.

And, thanks to the flier that had been shoved into my hand before the Dreamland show, I knew exactly where that particular performer would be later tonight.

CHAPTER 7

So why was I running across a bridge in the middle of the night? Well, if you've ever lived in Brooklyn, you're probably expecting a crack about the dismal service on the F Train, so consider it made. The rest of you won't have any idea what that last sentence means, but trust me; it's *hi*larious. (Unless you're reading this while waiting for a subway at the Second Avenue Station at 3:00 A.M. In that case, it's just plain depressing.)

The smells coming out of Danny's Deep-Fry were either delicious or disgusting, and I wasn't sure which yet. I suspected that, even if it were the former, prolonged exposure to the scent would quickly convert it to the latter. And since I was about to walk into the place, prolonged exposure was unavoidable. The dive bar & grill was located on one of those side streets near City Hall which—since most of Manhattan south of TriBeCa clears out after the post-work drinking hour—is not a great neighborhood for nightlife. But intrepid yet inexperienced entrepreneurs keep opening bars, trying, failing, and selling their businesses to the next group of intrepid yet inexperienced entrepreneurs. This particular destined-to-close venture appeared, at street level, to be a simple downmarket BBQ joint, the kind that (in the right part of the country) would be surprisingly good eatin' despite the decor. In the financial district of Manhattan it was more likely to be surprisingly greasy. At best. It claimed to also be a performance space, and cited as evidence of that fact a stage in a basement that had all the grace and charm of an Elk's Club rec room in South Jersey.

Exactly the sort of place in which Angelina Blood would never be caught dead, let alone perform. But Krash played in a heavy metal band, which for obvious reasons took whatever gigs it could get. And in those first romantic months of a relationship—a state, based on their behavior last night, that I was guessing they were in—you support your significant other in any way you can. Which meant that when I walked down those stairs I was treated to the sight of Angelina, with her raven-black hair, nails, clothing, and eyes, delightfully situated against a red-and-white checkered vinyl tablecloth and the wood-paneled basement walls of Danny's Deep-Fry.

Much to my dismay—and by "dismay," I mean "relief"—I walked into that basement just as Krash and her band were breaking down. It wasn't an accident. I had added an hour to the start time on the flier, hoping to schedule my arrival to miss the gig but catch Angelina. My timing was perfect. She sat alone at a table, watching the band as they packed up their instruments. Those black eyes were more glazed than I had seen them previously.

I sat down opposite her.

"Hi," I said.

Angelina looked at me.

"I'd like to talk to you. About last night."

She stared at me.

"I'm talking to everybody in the show. Not just you."

She continued to stare at me.

"I know it was tough, with Victoria doing your number and all. I understand that you might not want to talk about it."

Angelina stared.

"But here's the thing—it turns out that you might have been the only person other than me to have access to Victoria's suitcase. So it's probably in your best interest to answer a couple of questions."

Angelina kept right on staring. I don't think she had blinked once since I sat down. But her eyes flicked to the left, over my shoulder. I turned my head to find Krash behind me, a bit too close for comfort, wearing a denim vest that displayed a pair of rather impressively muscular arms. The scowl on her face was accentuated by the blue mohawk.

The other four members of her band stood with her.

"This guy bothering you, Angel?" Krash said.

Angelina stared at me.

Krash interpreted that to mean yes.

"Come on, buddy, let's take it outside." She grabbed my collar and lifted me to my feet.

"I'm not—" I started.

"You wanna walk out of here? 'Cause I can drag you." Krash said. The four guys behind her nodded in unison.

Angelina stared at me.

"Look, I—" I said.

"I said *now*, punk," said Krash, and pushed me toward

the stairwell. She hadn't actually said 'now' (at least until now), but I didn't correct her. Discretion is the better part of not getting your ass kicked by a heavy metal band. Plus, my arm still ached from my earlier ejection from the strip club, so I had a vested interest in making this particular exit under my own power.

I glanced over my shoulder at Angelina as I started up the steps.

She blinked.

On the sidewalk in front of Danny's Deep-Fry, I tried to reason with Krash and her band, with exactly as much success as you might expect.

I explained that I was just asking a few questions of the people who had been there last night, nothing serious, not accusing, just asking. I offered to ask Krash a few questions, too, if she liked, to prove my sincerity.

Krash thought about it for a moment, ran a hand through her Mohawk, and punched me in the stomach.

Another band member—the biggest one—grabbed my collar and led me down the street, where all the stores were closed and foot traffic was nonexistent. Krash walked with us, hitting me in the arm every couple of steps, each punch slightly harder than the last. The other three members of the band tagged along behind.

I was starting to get the feeling that this conversation was not going to go well. It was time to extract myself from the situation, in the most expedient manner possible.

Lucky for me, I was wearing, as I often do, a shirt

that fastened with snaps rather than buttons. I prefer shirts with snaps. Makes them easier to remove quickly, which is a plus in my line of work. And you never know when a piece of clothing from your wardrobe will make its way into a number.

Ease of removal was a plus tonight, too. I lunged forward, tearing the shirt open as I did, and ran, leaving the garment in the hands of my escort. And I kept running, across Broadway, towards City Hall. The park was closed this time of night, but the winding pathway between the Tweed Courthouse and City Hall stays open later. If I made pursuit difficult enough, maybe the drunken band members would decide they'd prefer to return to Danny's Deep-Fry and finish packing up their equipment, rather than chasing me around downtown.

As I passed the cluster of concrete chess tables that lined the path, I shot a glance behind me. Had my plan worked? No such luck. All five were sprinting across Broadway towards me. I had a good head start, but Krash and the biggest one were beginning to catch up. And they looked like they were enjoying themselves. Great. They'd gotten themselves all riled for a pummeling, and they weren't going to give up their punching bag just because it was running away.

I popped out of the pathway and into the wide pedestrian mall on the other side of City Hall. I glanced around, assessing my escape options. From this vantage point, I could see four choices nearby:

Option 1: The 6 train. There was an entrance to my left. Now, in almost every movie, TV show, or after-school special ever written about New York by an L.A. writer from Ohio, the escapee running away tries to elude capture by ducking into a subway station. This is something no self-respecting New Yorker would ever do. Look, it's *the subway*. When you get into the station, you're going to have to *wait for it to arrive*. For *at least* 10 minutes. On the same platform *as the people chasing you*.

This is not a viable escape plan.

Option 2: Downtown, via Park Row. Not a chance. Like I said, the financial district shuts down after dark, and is full of twists, turns, and delightfully dark alleys in which I could be beaten up with impunity.

Option 3: Uptown on Centre Street, similarly abandoned at this time of night. Where, just a couple of blocks north, there was a park perfectly situated for a quiet and unobserved pummeling.

Option 4: Brooklyn. Across the street from me was the pedestrian ramp to the Brooklyn Bridge. Sure, getting all the way across would be a bit of a hike, but I figured no one in their right mind (and certainly no one who'd left all their instruments at a venue called Danny's Deep-Fry) was going to chase me across an entire river and into a different borough.

You've already seen how well that worked out.

CHAPTER 8

So, there I was, four and a half minutes later, halfway across the Brooklyn Bridge, half-naked and completely out of breath.

The porkpie that the breeze had taken off my head was lying a dozen or so feet away, directly in the path of the oncoming horde of hair-metal rockers. Krash, her mohawk flapping from side to side as she ran, and the big guy—who still had my shirt clutched in his hand—were quite a bit ahead of the rest of the band. Even at this distance, it was clear that the three bringing up the rear were several beers worse for wear.

To hell with it.

I like that hat.

I ran directly at them, screaming my lungs out, hoping the element of surprise would shake them.

They weren't surprised. Amused, maybe. Not surprised. I had forgotten that I was dealing with people who probably pulled this sort of maneuver all the time.

The big one was in the lead. He leapt over my hat and we barreled toward each other on a collision course. At the last minute, I dropped my shoulder and hit the ground rolling. Hair Metal did the instinctual thing and jumped. I tumbled under him and popped back up onto my feet, grabbing my pork-pie as I did so.

Ow. That sort of thing didn't hurt as much when I was a teenager.

But I had my hat back. I also had a problem. Because the slower three members of the band were catching up. The faster two had turned around after I rolled past them, and were heading back in my direction. Which meant I had made myself lunch meat in a heavy metal sandwich.

I pulled my hat down, as tightly as possible, over my long, beautiful hair.

I was surrounded. And even if I could find some way to break away, there was a stitch in my side telling me I wasn't currently in any shape to outrun even the drunkest rocker in the band.

I glanced around. Couldn't go forward, couldn't go backward. There was only one way I could go. One place I didn't think they would follow me.

To my right and left were the railings that separate the wooden walkway in the center of the Brooklyn Bridge from the cars on either side. The pedestrian path is raised a couple dozen feet above the inbound and outbound vehicular traffic, to make life more dif-ficult for potential jumpers, I suppose. You'd have to be fairly committed to crawl across a steel girder and over three lanes of speeding traffic just to make a dra-matic leap into the East River.

I was fairly committed. Not to suicide, but to putting some distance between my body and the fists of Krash and her crew. I backed away as they advanced, making sure my ass was pointed in the direction of one of the railings. When butt hit wood, I hopped the railing as smoothly as my aching muscles could manage, turned my back on the band, and walked out onto one of the steel girders.

My attempt to remain upright lasted exactly two steps before I dropped to all fours and started crawling.

The girder was cold under my hands. My hands were sweating. The sweat was cold. The rivets hurt my knees. Whine, whine, whine. I crept forward, slowly, slowly. Below me, the late-night traffic was mostly taxis—yellow cabs, car services—and those drivers didn't slow down for anything. I tried not to look. If the fall didn't kill me, there'd be no dearth of speeding livery to finish the job.

The breeze picked up. Wind whistled past my ears. *Wow*, it seemed to be saying, *you're a moron*.

I chanced a look over my shoulder. Krash and the band were standing at the railing, watching me crawl.

"Fuck, yeah," said the guitarist. Well, one of the guitarists. From what I'd seen of their instruments, I estimated that there were four in the band. Anyway, the big guitarist. The one with my shirt. He stepped over the railing onto the girder. And started walking toward me.

Once again, I had underestimated the stupidity of an idiot.

I need to stop making mistakes like that.

The guitarist was walking the girder like a tightrope. And catching up.

This was turning into a problem. If they'd caught me on the bridge, or in the park, they probably would have skinned their knuckles on my face a little and that would have been that. A few bruises, maybe a black eye, a broken rib or two at worst. Nothing permanent. But if I was going to be facing off with a heavy metal rocker with no instinct for self preservation on a narrow steel girder twenty feet above a cascading automotive death river, not to mention two hundred feet above a cascading watery death river, my chances of fatality had grown exponentially.

I decided not to mention this to Filthy.

And I kept crawling. As I did, I attempted to reason with him.

"Hey"—I said over my shoulder as I went—"why don't we head back to the middle of the bridge and hang out? Or, you know, whatever it is we were planning to do before we got on this girder. I'll turn around if you will!"

He grinned and kept walking towards me.

Bright kid.

And then, suddenly, there I was, at the end of my girder. Right on the edge of the Brooklyn Bridge. My options had suddenly dwindled to a) down, b) far down, and c) extremely far down (and quite wet). My friend was about a third of the way across, but he was closing the gap.

Now would be an excellent time to think of something clever. Like, oh, I don't know, maybe I could jump onto the roof of a speeding taxi. On the other hand, smashing my head repeatedly against the girder would probably achieve the same basic effect with significantly less effort.

"Hey, look," I said, pointing out over the water toward the Manhattan skyline. "The Chrysler Building!"

The guitarist looked, nodded, shrugged. And kept coming.

Well, there went that plan. Whatever it was. I looked around to see if I could come up with any other brilliant ideas.

And I did. Well, not brilliant, exactly. Fairly stupid, actually, when you got right down to it. But it was an idea.

Driving toward me on the roadway below was one of those damn tourist buses. The double-decker kind with open tops that drive across the bridge in the middle of the night to give camera-happy visitors to our fair city a chance to snap the sort of blurry memory of the Manhattan skyline one can only really achieve in a moving vehicle barreling across a bumpy bridge.

It was driving in the lane that would take it directly under me. Where it would offer a surface I could drop onto that was both considerably flatter and considerably closer than any other available option. No, it wasn't a smart thing to do, per se, but—but nothing. It wasn't a smart thing to do.

I was going to do it anyway.

I swung my legs over the side of the girder and let myself down, keeping my arms tightly wrapped around the cold metal. My pursuer was about halfway across. The wind had picked up again and even given the lack of regard for his own life he had so far displayed, he was forced to move more slowly.

Please don't change lanes. Please don't change lanes.

I could see the faces of the tourists on the upper level of the bus as it approached. They seemed vaguely interested. Vaguely. Hey, a man hanging from a girder is great and all, but isn't that the Empire State Building just over the water?

I lowered myself until I was hanging just by my hands. My legs kicked in the air. Damn it, my palms had never been this sweaty. If I lost my grip and dropped in front of the bus instead of on top of it…well, at least it would make an amusing obituary.

The bus rattled closer. The guy behind me on the girder got closer, too. It was a coin toss which would get to me first. I could hear the tour guide, standing with his back to me, saying into a microphone, "In 1885, Robert E. Odlum was the first person to jump off the Brooklyn Bridge, plunging…"

That was as good a cue as any. The bus was directly under me now. I lifted my legs to avoid kicking the tour guide in the head, then let go of the girder.

I dropped into the aisle, hitting it exactly as planned, between the rows of seats on either side. What I hadn't planned on was physics: the forward momentum of the bus swept me off my feet and I went head over heels down the aisle. I tumbled forward, narrowly missing the steps leading down to the lower level, landing finally at the back end of the bus with my head on the floor and my feet in the lap of a rather surprised-looking elderly gentleman.

Not the most graceful performance of my career, but at least I was on the bus and not under it.

Over the grey hair of the man whose pants my shoes were currently dirtying I could see the guitarist standing in the middle of the girder, watching the bus drive away. I winked at him as he receded into the distance. He probably couldn't see it.

I rolled backward, popped to my feet, and adjusted my porkp—oh, crap. Where was my hat?

The porkpie lay at the feet of the tour guide, marking the spot in the aisle onto which I had dropped. As I started forward to retrieve it, the wind took it instead and blew it up into the air.

I reached out and grabbed.

And this time, I caught it.

I donned the hat and bent the front of the rim down. You know, for style. I smiled at the blue-haired couple next to me. Then I reached into my back pocket and handed them—oh, yes, I always carry a few with me—a postcard for my next show. They looked at it, smiled, nodded, and looked generally confused.

A woman in front of me leaned over and whispered to her companion, "I betcha the bus company organized that. Happens every trip, I betcha."

The companion shook her head, and said, "Only in New York. Only in New York."

I hate people who say that.

❖

The F Train wasn't running.

It took me another two hours to get home.

I crawled into bed next to Filthy.

"Tomorrow you can pretend to be a fireman!" she mumbled.

I ignored her.

CHAPTER 9
FRIDAY

Oh, god, Times Square. That neon-encrusted, advertising-infested, flickering heart of New York; seedy before they gussied it up at the end of the last century, but with a certain gut-wrenching charm. Even seedier now, though in a different way. Not as run down, but run out. No cleaner, though mopped. No safer, though patrolled. No better, though upgraded. Like one of those Atlantic City casinos that was redecorated instead of being destroyed, but without the gambling to offset the depressive tackiness of the decor. Offering the same wealth of shopping possibilities available at your least favorite mall and all the crowded charm of your least favorite riot. Times Square: the pop-up ad in the center of Manhattan.

I can't believe people still have offices here.

I woke up aching and battered, but doggedly determined to finish my conversation of the previous night. Because, let's face it, I wasn't exactly thrilled about the way my interview with Angelina Blood had played out. So I wanted to talk to her again—this time, for more than three minutes, and in a place where she didn't have backup.

I knew just the place. A location in which she'd

have to be polite, would have to talk to me. I happened to be in possession of the knowledge that Angelina Blood…

…had a day job.

Some do. We don't hold it against them.

The corporate world was just as I remembered it, a symphony of shared desks, dead faces, tired hands tapping away at keyboards, an occasional surreptitious glance out the window, at the clock, or at that other employee you fantasize is someday going to invite you for an erotic tête-à-tête in the supply closet.

It filled me with a dread I had not had the displeasure of experiencing since those first few months out of college, when I returned to New York and tried to settle back into the city of my birth in a profession that didn't involve taking off my clothes.

It was a mistake. I'd made my first entrance in this city naked and kicking, and that was clearly the way this city wanted me to stay.

That error was soon rectified, by mutual acrimonious agreement, and I managed to collect a none-too-generous severance package in the process of getting myself fired…but that's another story.

The elevator doors opened to reveal a reception desk. The young woman behind it was on the phone, so I stepped out and waited for her to finish.

"Welcome to—oh." The receptionist broke off when she saw my face.

It's a good thing Angelina recognized me, because I sure as hell wouldn't have recognized her. Her raven black hair was still there, sure, but it was wrapped up at the back of her head in a corporate little bun. Her eyes, which I was seeing for the first time without alteration, were bright blue, made all the brighter by being framed in a pair of tortoiseshell horn-rimmed glasses. She completed the look with a rather snappy little grey suit.

It was just the cutest secretary drag I had ever seen. I had to stifle a laugh. Burlesque performers are so good at dressing up, she actually almost fit the surroundings. Except for the look in her eyes. Blue though they were, the eyes—and the anger in them—belonged to the Angelina I knew.

"Hello," I said.

"Can I help you…sir?" She pronounced the word "sir" as if it rhymed with "go fuck yourself."

"Yes, I'm very interested in the world of"—I glanced at the sign on the wall behind her—"trade magazine fulfillment services. Could you tell me a little more about it?"

She smiled and hissed through clenched teeth, "Kiss my ass."

"You know, Angelina—" She hissed again, and shook her head. Ah, she used another name at the office. That was a helpful bit of information, since I was probably going to need a lever of some sort to get her to talk to me. "I have to admit that I'm not kindly disposed toward you after last night. I've recently come down with a bad case of being a murder suspect, and getting chased across a bridge by a bunch of heavy metal hooligans didn't exactly help my symptoms. So I—as a person who was so terribly inconvenienced by your friends and loved ones, or at least by your loved one's friends—would very much like to ask you now the questions I wanted to ask you last night."

Angelina glared at me, and shook her head.

"Really?" I said. "Really?" I raised my voice slightly, so it could be heard through the glass wall that separated the reception area from the rest of the office. "So you're telling me that if I went online, I could see *what* sort of pictures? Ooooh, I'd like to see *those*. They sound like *fun*. What was that web address again? W...w...w...dot... angelinab—"

Angelina hissed. She jerked her head down a fraction of an inch—making sure I could see the effort it cost her—and then back up. It was as close to a nod as I was going to get from her.

"Good," I said, dropping my voice to a whisper. "Let's talk about Wednesday night. You got to Topkapi early. Was Krash with you when you got there?"

Angelina nodded again.

"Fine. You put your bag in the alcove. Or did Krash do it for you?"

Angelina shook her head.

"You did it yourself. Was there another bag there?"

Angelina nodded again.

"Did you happen to peek inside that other bag?"

Angelina just glared.

I sighed. This interview wasn't going to offer nearly as much entertainment value as Eva's. But at least what Angelina was saying—if you could call it "saying"— seemed to confirm what I'd figured out based on Eva's account, namely that Victoria's bag must have arrived at the venue before Victoria had. Which meant the list of possible suspects had just gotten a whole lot longer...and the person now at the top of it was the person with whom I was currently speaking. She'd just admitted to spending some quality time alone with the bag in question, and if she had peeked inside, she would have had every reason in the world to be upset by its contents. But had she? If she had been snooping, she sure as hell wasn't going to tell me. I decided to press some buttons and see what came out.

"I hate to tell you this," I lied, "but you've got a serious problem. As long as the cops thought that Victoria arrived at the venue with her suitcase in tow, they figured I was the only one who could have tampered with the bottle. But you just confirmed that her bag was at Topkapi before I even walked in the door. And that you had every opportunity to examine it and tamper with the contents before anyone else showed up."

Angelina's voice was quiet. "You're trying to frame me?"

"I'm just telling you what the cops are going to think."

"You're setting me up. Trying to make it look like I killed a girl I never even met before that night."

"You never met her? She stole your number."

"Which I found out for the first time that night when I saw her do it. You're not going to pin this crap on me, Porkpie." She spoke so passionately that for a moment I could almost believe she was innocent. "I'm not going to let you. I don't care what convoluted crap you're dreaming up to cover your own ass, but I'll stab you in the eye before I let you put me in jail."

Okay, that last part didn't seem quite as innocent.

"I'm not trying to frame you, Angelina. I'm just trying to find out who killed Victoria."

"Who cares?" she hissed.

"Let me give you a sampling of the questions the cops are going to ask you, now that you're a suspect. First off, they're going to want to know why you decided to do that particular number on that particular night."

"And I'll tell them," Angelina said. "That I did it because LuLu told me not to."

"Do you really think they're going to believe—wait, what?"

"LuLu never liked that number. She told me I could do any other number I wanted at Dreamland, but not that one, not at her show. She hated that one."

"And you were going to do it anyway?"

"She wasn't there."

"Wow. That's…not very professional."

"Oh, please."

"Oh, please, yourself." Now I was annoyed. "If a producer doesn't like an act of yours, you don't perform that act at their show. Especially not on a night where the producer isn't there." That sort of behavior reeked of grade school antics, 'look what I can do when teacher's back is turned.' "That's bush league," I said. "You had to know LuLu would find out, and she never would have booked you again."

She glared at me some more. "What makes you think I *wanted* to perform for her again?"

Grade school again. This was nice. We were really building up a delightful dislike of each other, served with side order of suspicion.

Behind me, the elevator bell dinged.

I heard someone get out and saw Angelina look past my shoulder. Her face relaxed. She beckoned the person over and rolled her eyes in my direction.

"This guy bothering you, Emily?" said a disturbingly familiar voice.

Angelina—Emily—smiled. It was the first real smile I had seen on her face. I had a sneaking suspicion that whatever was making her happy would have exactly the opposite effect on me.

I turned around.

There was a large fellow behind me. His hair was pulled tightly back in a ponytail rather than hanging loose, but I recognized him immediately. Because this particular large fellow was the same large fellow I had last seen twelve hours earlier standing on a crossbeam of the Brooklyn Bridge.

He was wearing a uniform with the words "Universal Security" emblazoned in bright yellow on the chest pocket.

"Jonny," Angelina said, in a sickly sweet voice, "I'd like to introduce you to my friend Brian. He works at the security desk downstairs. Brian, this is Jonny Porkpie. Oh! But you two have already met, haven't you?"

Brian held out a meaty palm.

I wasn't falling for that trick. I'd seen too many

drunks escorted out of bars by a handshake from a bouncer that turned into an arm twisted behind the back.

"Nice to see you again," I said, smiling and keeping my arms firmly at my sides.

Though it remained unshaken, Brian's hand was continuing to move in my direction in a manner that could only be described as 'threatening.'

I decided that my interview with Angelina had come to an end.

As Brian made a grab for my shoulder, I ducked under his hand and scooted into the elevator just as the doors were closing.

CHAPTER 10

It wasn't exactly how I'd wanted that interview to end, but I was at least a bit further along than I had been when I woke up this morning. I now had a better sense of who could have tampered with the prop bottle in Victoria's bag: anyone. Anyone in the world—or at least anyone who'd been in the East Village before the Dreamland show began on Wednesday night. And two more questions had been raised: how long had Victoria's bag been in that alcove before I arrived, and who had put it there?

As important as those questions were, though, there was still the one that trumped them: Who had tampered with the bottle? It was possible that it had happened before I arrived, maybe even before Angelina had, and I'd look into that possibility if I had to, but I already knew for a fact that there were several beautiful women who had spent time alone behind the curtain with that bag, when they'd dropped off their own suitcases in the alcove. And those women already happened to be my most likely suspects. Two of them I had already spoken to. Two remained. I could have flipped a coin, I suppose, but I figured I might as well start with the woman to whom I owed a thank you.

For the loan of her pet lawyer.

*

I'd never been to Jillian's dungeon before. When I called her to see if she had time to chat with me, she said she would be tied up there all afternoon—sorry, that's not entirely accurate; she said she would be tying people up there all afternoon. But she said I should feel free to drop by.

It wasn't actually a dungeon, not in the classical— or rather, Medieval—sense of the word. The room I walked into when she opened the door wasn't dank and mildewed with stone walls and iron chains as the only decoration. The walls were covered in red velvet, and the chains hanging from them were, if I was to hazard a guess, reinforced steel.

But as a place to conduct an interrogation, it had a certain charm.

"Nice decor," I said, as I sat down on a divan uphol-stered in the same red velvet as the walls.

"Yeah, cheesy, right? But it's what the clients expect." Jillian wore a robe over what looked like a tight-fitting, low-cut leather bustier. The outfit went well with the room.

"So," I said. "I wanted to thank you for the loan of your lawyer friend."

"Don't ever mention that again," Jillian said, in a voice I imagined she usually reserved for her clients. It was only momentary, though, and with the next sen-tence her tone was that of the Jillian I knew. "But you're welcome. Hey, do you want a cup of tea?"

"Sure," I said, and she vanished through the door. I heard her footsteps receding into the depths of the establishment.

While she was gone, I took a stroll around the room. Never having been in a working dungeon before, I was curious. The chains were the real thing, heavy and serious-looking. At one station there was a manacle for each hand, the height adjustable, it seemed, based on whether you wanted the client's feet touching the floor or not. For those feet, there was a pair of shackles right above the molding. All of these were securely attached to the wall—*very* securely attached. I pulled on one of them and estimated that they could, with very little strain, support the full weight of a man twice my size.

There was a cabinet in the corner of the room. Locked. I'd seen Jillian integrate some of the tools of the trade into her acts, so I had some idea what was inside, but just for fun I spent a couple of seconds imagining what might be behind those doors that was too risqué even for burlesque.

Aside from the divan and the cabinet, the room's only furniture was a plain wooden folding chair that seemed sort of out of place, but I'm sure it had its uses. The hardwood floor seemed out of place, too—I might have expected a deep shag carpet with that wallpaper—but I guessed the wood was easier to clean.

Jillian came back bearing a tray with a small pink tea set, which she set down on the top of the cabinet. She poured, and handed me a cup.

"Thanks," I said. "So, listen, I'm here because I wanted to talk about…"

"Bottoms up," she said, raising her teacup. I'm never one to turn down a toast, even if it's just tea.

"Likewise," I said, and drained the cup. I put it on

the tray, and she poured me another. "Strange taste," I said. "Lapsang souchong?"

"No. Private blend. Now, you wanted to talk about something?" Strange, I thought: Jillian hadn't touched her tea. And she likes tea. A lot. But instead of drinking it, she seemed to be pouring her cup back into the pot.

"The, uh—" The steam coming out of my own tea-cup was fascinating. It was making the most interesting twists and swirls. "Wednesday night at Dreamland…" Behind the steam, Jillian's bustier was getting more obvious. Oh, that was because she had taken off her robe. It was black, like I said before, black leather. "—murder at the, Victoria and—" She was also wearing black boots, I noticed. With high heels. High, high, sharp heels. "—police were, think I'm the—" Strange, I hadn't noticed her boots before. Why was I noticing them now? Oh! Because I was on the floor. That's funny —why was I on the floor? I guess it didn't matter. Those boots mattered, though. They were black, like I said, and very tall, and black and shiny—oh, wait, no they weren't, they were black and blurry. Come to think of it, everything was black. What was I talking about? Oh, yes. Dreamland.

I opened my eyes. Or did I? I still couldn't see anything. Huh. Weird. I blinked a few times, as a test. Yep, my eyes were as wide open as a pervert's fly just before he gets himself kicked out of a burlesque show. But my eyelashes were hitting something rough each time I blinked. My guess was that the something rough was the thing preventing me from seeing.

I reached for it and—and nothing. I couldn't reach for it. My arm wouldn't move. Something was holding it in place. I tried the other arm. Nope. Tried to move my legs. No luck there, either.

This was somewhat disconcerting.

I wasn't dead, at least. I knew that for a fact, because I could feel a draft. Although I can't say that I was at all optimistic about where I was feeling it.

"Oh, Jonny, Jonny, Jonny," said a voice. I knew that voice. That was Jillian's voice. I heard a door close. I heard a lock lock. I heard high heels click-clack across the hardwood floor, getting louder as they came in my direction.

Something brushed against my cheek.

I felt fingernails on the back of my head.

Suddenly, the world exploded into light.

Jillian dangled the blindfold in front of me as my eyes adjusted to the brightness of the room.

"Sorry to keep you waiting," she said, "A client dropped in just before you arrived. I had to finish him off before we could...chat."

"No worries," I said. "I've just been—"

"If you say 'hanging around,' Jonny, I swear to god I will whip you."

It was an idle threat, and I knew it. She wasn't going to whip me. She didn't even have a whip. That thing in her hand was a riding crop.

"—here," I finished. I figured it was a good idea to play it safe, at least until Jillian's intentions were clearer. It's not every day you wake up shackled to a friend's wall.

"Mmm-hm. So. Jonny. Jonny, Jonny, Jonny." Jillian

caressed my cheek with the riding crop, then ran it down my body to—well, let's just say the areas further down my body. She continued: "You came here to accuse me of murder, didn't you?"

I chuckled. I shook my head. "Don't be silly. No. No, that isn't it at all. What I came here to do was ask you some questions. Questions about Victoria's death, yes, but to accuse you of murder? I'm in no position to do any such a thing." Certainly not at the moment. "Just asking questions, is all."

"So ask 'em."

I glanced down.

"Like this?"

Jillian shrugged and lowered herself onto the divan. She began untying those boots I had noticed earlier, when I was passing out on the floor. It wasn't going to be quick—each boot started just below her knee and went all the way down, and had the laces to prove it.

"I should mention, Jillian," I said, "that in the grand scheme of things, this looks a little suspicious."

"What does?"

"Me. Wall. Shackles. Lack of pants, shirt, shoes, socks, or indeed any other clothing-related accoutrements."

"Does it?" Jillian seemed unconcerned. She continued her work with the bootlaces. At least she had put down the riding crop.

"Well, I mean, look at it," I said. "I arrive here, you offer me a cup of tea—"

"Tea!" she exclaimed. "Thank you for reminding me. I didn't get to have any earlier." She stood up and left. How she managed to walk so quickly in heels that high with bootlaces half-untied was beyond me.

With Jillian out of the room again, I took a moment to consider my situation. It wasn't exactly what I would describe as promising. I was trussed up better than a freshman pledge during a frat initiation. The chains showed no signs of wanting to come out of the wall. The leather restraints around my wrists and ankles could be unbuckled if I happened to have a hand free. But I didn't. I clenched my muscles and pulled…no leeway whatsoever. Jillian knew her business.

But let's see…

If I could just reach that buckle with one finger, just a single finger, I might be able to…

Nope.

I bent my wrist until it hurt and didn't get within a fingernail of the thing.

Maybe I could slide a hand out of the restraint. The skin was certainly sweaty enough. If I just squeezed my fingers together and pulled with all my strength…

By the time Jillian returned a few minutes later, I had managed to wedge my hand so firmly into the shackle that I was unable to move it in either direction, in or out.

She sat on the divan, poured herself some tea, took a sip, and then resumed the process of unlacing her boot.

"So, you were saying?" she said.

What had I been saying? Oh, right. "I was saying, don't you think this looks suspicious? I take a few sips of tea, next thing I know, I wake up naked and strapped to your wall."

"You came to a pro domme and wound up in chains? I

don't think anyone would consider that suspicious," she
said. She called out over her shoulder, to the closed door
behind her, "For crying out loud, are you ready yet?"

"Me?" I said.

"Not you, silly. You're ready for whatever I tell you
you're ready for."

From the other side of the door came a negative-
sounding grunt.

Jillian sighed. "Looks like we have a couple minutes
to kill, Jonny. What did you want to talk about?"

"You mean, other than who's on the other side of
that door?"

"Yeah, that would be telling."

"Well, all right," I said. "Let's talk about Victoria,
then."

"What do you want to know?"

"To start, what happened between the two of you,"
I said. "The rumor going around was that you were
pissed because she opened up a burlesque school and
you thought yours should be the only one."

"Yeah, guess who spread *that* rumor," Jillian said,
after downing some more tea. "That's not why I was
pissed. You want to open a burlesque school? Go for
it. Be my guest. I don't own the idea. But I do own
the materials I created for *my* school. And when she
opened hers, in Philly? Guess what she handed out to
her students."

"Your materials?" I said.

"She covered up my name and wrote in her own.
That was the extent of her original work. I had a lawyer
friend (who shall remain nameless and about whom

we shall never speak again) draft a cease-and-desist, and she ceased. And desisted. And then," Jillian said, "started saying I was an arrogant bitch who claimed the exclusive right to teach burlesque on the East Coast. Now, I may be an arrogant bitch—but I don't claim any such thing. Hell, other people teach burlesque in New York City, you don't see me sending lawyers after them."

"So she made you pretty mad?" I said.

She smiled a sly smile. "Mad enough to kill her— that's where you're headed, right?"

"Not at all," I said, "just—"

"A month or so ago, I found out that she'd started using my handouts again. This time I just let it go. First off, I had revised them since, and who cares if someone is using your old crap? And second of all, by now everyone in the business knows what she is. It wasn't worth my time even to send her another C&D—you think it would've been worth it to kill her? I mean—"

She was interrupted by a knock at the door.

"Ah, finally," Jillian said. "Yes, he's all set," she continued. Then, as the door opened, "What took you so long?"

Filthy stood in the doorway in an outfit that I can't describe, because there wasn't enough of it to warrant description. Suffice to say, north of a pair of high-heeled boots almost identical to the ones Jillian was now holding in her hands, Filthy wore nothing that wasn't black, made of vinyl, and skin-tight. Her couture didn't provide much in the way of coverage, but let's be fair: it did beat what I was wearing.

"Are you kidding?" Filthy said. "Took me half an hour just to lace one boot."

"Well, he's all yours," Jillian said. "Don't do anything I wouldn't do." She sauntered out of the room, then turned around and looked back. "For the record, there's *nothing* I wouldn't do." She closed the door behind her. Filthy locked it.

I arranged my face into as judgmental a look as a man hanging naked on a wall can manage.

"Darling," I said. "I'm sure that whatever you have planned will be fun, but I should remind you that I am currently under suspicion of murder. Now is hardly the right time for this sort of thing."

"Actually, it's precisely the time. I'm not here for kicks—though I have to admit, seeing you like this does make me tingle in ways I enjoy immensely. But I'm here to prove a point."

"That you look hot in skin-tight vinyl? I could have told you that."

"That you, my dearest, are putting yourself at rather a lot of risk. What if Jillian were the murderer?"

"What if she *was*. Grammar, darling."

"What if she *were*—look it up, subjunctive case—and I weren't here? You wouldn't be chained to a wall, you'd be floating in the East River."

"Fine. Point taken. I'll be more careful in the future. I've learned my lesson."

"Oh, honey," Filthy said, picking up the riding crop. "We haven't even *started* the lesson."

CHAPTER 11

The sun was setting over Manhattan as I emerged from the subway station onto the streets of downtown Brooklyn. I still had a hike ahead of me, so I tried LuLu LaRue's number for the third time, but still without luck.

Eventually, Filthy had let me go. She'd had to. She couldn't keep me chained to Jillian's wall forever—Jillian had other clients, for one thing, and needed the dungeon back. Filthy had tried her best to convince me to abandon my inquiries, and made her point quite...enthusiastically. But I just wasn't ready to give it up, not when the cops seemed only interested in closing the case as quickly as possible using the most convictable suspect—me. If I didn't figure out who killed Victoria, who would?

As a compromise, I promised Filthy I'd be more careful, and wouldn't put myself at risk needlessly; in return, Filthy promised that if I got myself killed, her eulogy would consist of four words: "I told you so." But she unlocked the shackles. When you've been married as long as we have, you have a pretty good sense of when you're not going to win an argument, even if you're the one with the riding crop in your hand.

Given a choice, I prefer not to worry Filthy. I didn't

have a choice. And anyway, there was only one suspect left. If the first four interviews hadn't gotten me killed, how bad could the fifth one be?

Brioche à Tête lived and worked in a run-down industrial loft building with a bunch of other dancers, the kind of building not zoned for residential use that landlords rent out illicitly to artists for a few years to perk up a sagging neighborhood. As soon as the artists have raised the cachet of the area enough to make it fashionable ("the next Soho," the realtor listings will say), the landlords anonymously tip off the cops about the illegal tenants and the artists are evicted to make way for people who are willing to pay a premium to appear fashionable and live around the artistic vibe. The artistic vibe, of course, is busy carting all of its crap to the next run-down industrial loft in the next sagging neighborhood, which will be on a slightly less accessible subway line.

I'd never been to Brioche's building before, but I knew the neighborhood pretty well. I'd helped more than a few friends move out of it. I managed to slip in the front door as someone was coming out. I looked enough like the other residents of the building that she let me in without question. I was playing it safe, as promised—by not ringing up from the lobby, I was giving Brioche as little advance warning as possible, and therefore as little opportunity to plan my murder, if she was inclined in that direction.

To get to the higher floors, the building offered a freight elevator, nothing more than a platform with a metal gate on either side, hand-operated because it hadn't been upgraded since it the day it was installed. I pushed the lever down and the thing jerked into motion, creaking and groaning as it ascended.

I closed my eyes for a moment on the way up. It had been an exhausting couple of days, and I was operating on even less sleep than usual. I opened them again to discover that I had passed Brioche's floor. I pulled the lever in the other direction. The elevator clattered to a stop and started down with a lurch that left my stomach on the level above. Even though I was paying attention this time, it took me a few tries to get the elevator aligned with Brioche's landing. When I did, I pulled the gate out of the way and knocked on Brioche's door.

She opened it naked. Completely naked.

"Oh," I said. "Sorry. Were you in the middle of rehearsing or something?"

"No," she said. "Come in. I was just about to make tea. Would you like some?"

"Thanks," I said. "No. Have you been speaking to my wife, by any chance?"

"Why do you ask?" she said, cocking her head to one side. She gestured toward a large open area to her left. "Please, sit."

I looked around the room. Except for a small braided rug in the exact center of the hardwood floor, there wasn't a stick of furniture. So I sat on the rug. Brioche sat opposite me.

"I'm not in a rush," I said. "If you want to put on a robe or something."

"You've seen me in this state dozens of times,

Jonny Porkpie. I hardly think it necessary to cover myself in my own house in deference to a societal conception of modesty to which neither I nor you subscribe. Had I been uncomfortable in your presence, I would have clothed myself before opening the door. Besides, it's too damn hot in here. Feel free to join me if you like."

I thanked her but demurred. She cocked her head at me and looked me in the eyes. I looked back, but the mottled blue told me nothing—as usual—of what she might be thinking.

"I can only assume," Brioche said, "that you've dropped in to discuss the events of this past Wednesday. No doubt you have already been informed by someone that I am, as you are, among the people who bore a measure of personal, one might even say spiritual, animosity towards Victoria, an animosity that was expiated to some degree, though not entirely expunged, by her death."

"Yes," I said.

"To which of the major schools of twentieth century psychology do you subscribe, Jonny Porkpie? Structuralism? Behaviorism? Cognitive? Humanistic? Or are you of the school that conceives of the human psyche in a more philosophical manner?"

I replied that I had not yet chosen a school, but I planned to apply to several and see where I got in. Brioche smiled, to indicate that she was aware that I was attempting to be amusing.

"Well, whichever you end up embracing, most will tell you that I simply don't fit the archetype of a murderer. You, on the other hand, frequently display three out of the ten winsome attributes outlined in the writings of the Chinese philosopher—"

"What was your problem with Victoria?" I interrupted. A crash course in Chinese philosophy was not what I needed right now, especially if it was going to explain how I made a better murderer than she did.

"How shall I put this? You are, of course, aware of the underlying metaphor behind contemporary Swedish dramatist's Nypa Botten's earlier poetic works, taken as a whole. His version of the Personius myth—removing all references to Personious himself, of course—provides a reasonable analogy for the situation."

I had a sneaking suspicion that she was making this up as she went along. On the other hand, if anyone would have a working knowledge of obscure Nordic playwrights, it was Brioche. My best course was probably to try to play along. When the need arises, I can shovel it with the best of them. It got me through college.

"I fail," I bullshat, "to see how the parallel can be contextualized to a modern paradigm, but perhaps that's because we've yet to adequately define our terms. Perhaps you can clarify the essence of your metaphor in contemporary rhetoric?"

Brioche furrowed her brow, but not in a manner that suggested she thought what I'd said made no sense. Rather, her expression was one of serious consideration. "Contemplate if you will," she said at last, "the central image-slash-paradox of that fable, the conundrum of the lizard and the yew tree. An imperfect correlation, I admit, but to take a step back from it and regard instead a crumbling stone on a wall some three miles distant, and a blade of grass about to be crushed by a single drop of dew, that will give you some idea of how the situation developed."

I attempted to formulate an appropriate response, but found my ability to circumlocute had atrophied over the years. So it was back to the straightforward approach. "Are you telling me," I asked, "that you and Victoria used to be friends, but she screwed you over?"

"Hardly, Jonny Porkpie. Hardly. There was always a dissonance there."

"So she stole one of your acts?"

The look of disdain Brioche gave me would have wilted a block of concrete. "Have you even *read* Nypa?" she said.

"Not since kindergarten," I said. This was getting me nowhere. I decided it was time to try a different angle. A more practical angle. "Listen. When you arrived at Topkapi, you asked for someone to order you a drink while you went to stash your suitcase— white wine of some sort?"

"A blanc seems not implausible."

"You and the glass of wine showed up at the bar almost simultaneously, and we both know it takes a few minutes to get a drink at Topkapi. Tossing your bag into the alcove should be a matter of twenty seconds. So what took you so long? Were you looking in someone else's bag?" I dropped the question quickly, hoping to surprise her, and watched her face to see if her reaction gave anything away.

That reaction was a perplexed stare. Not very helpful. "Another person's bag? For what reason?"

"Any of several," I said.

"Such as…?"

"Such as, to discover which act she was planning to perform."

"Oh, I wouldn't do that, Jonny Porkpie. One must always respect the liminal space inherent in another artist's luggage."

"All right, then what *were* you doing that took you so long?"

"I think," she said. "Or rather, I seem to think…that I was talking to someone. Yes."

"Who?"

"An archetype. One of those who comes to shows reeking of sweat and desire. One who is by definition the definition of himself, and no more. He was lingering in the vicinity of the curtains. I'm always intrigued by the observations of such men on the art of burlesque. It's a perspective to which I do not often have access."

"And what were his observations?"

"If I remember correctly, he expressed an ardent appreciation for the specifics of the unclad feminine form."

"He said that?"

"Not exactly."

"What did he say exactly?"

"He said he liked the tits."

"Classy."

"Rather."

"What did this archetype look like?" I said.

"Archetypal. It was dark. I didn't absorb a lot of detail."

"In general terms, then."

"Sometimes a cloud will be split by the wing of a plane. A tangle of briars on a mountaintop. The drip of sordid rain."

"Less general than that."

"Are you familiar with the works of the Dutch Master von Snuifje?"

I shook my head.

"Were this man to have been painted, it would have been by von Snuifje. I'm sorry, but that's as specific as I can get."

She paused to consider.

"Oh," she said, "And he was wearing an overcoat."

Ah, yes. The creep in the overcoat.

As a pretext for her delay, it wasn't bad. I had seen the guy lurking by those curtains myself, and turned him away when he tried to follow us into the dressing room. And it would be just like Brioche to take an anthropological interest in one of the less palatable members of the burlesque audience.

Of course, she could be lying—she might have remembered my interaction with him at the door and seized on him as a convenient excuse. But then, it wouldn't be hard to track down a guy like this; based on his behavior, I had a feeling he was a frequent burlesque attendee. Since Saturday—bump and grind's busiest day of the week—was just around the corner, if

I didn't find him at one show, I'd find him at another. So her statement could be fairly easily proved or disproved, and she would know that. Which meant that for the time being I was going to assume she was telling the truth.

She was still a suspect; she could have tampered with the bottle then talked to the guy briefly to establish an alibi. But on further consideration, that scenario would have required a degree of calculation and practical thinking on Brioche's part that had not thus far been apparent in my interactions with her.

In other words, my final suspect, while not wholly in the clear, was as unpromising as the first four had—

It hit me then, like a poorly thrown brassiere.

Brioche wasn't my final suspect.

The man in the overcoat was.

The more I contemplated the idea, the more I wondered why I hadn't thought of it before. A suspicious-looking creep spending a suspicious amount of time right in the vicinity of the alcove where Victoria's bag was stashed? That same creep later sitting exactly where a murderer might sit if he wanted a front-row seat to the results of his handiwork? This guy seemed tailor made for the part of homicidal maniac, and I had been ignoring him entirely.

Granted, as a candidate for prime suspect, there were two problems with the creep. First, as far as I knew, he had no motive. It wasn't hard to conceive of possibilities—he was a jilted fan of Victoria; he was obsessed with one of the other performers in the show and exacting revenge on her behalf; so forth and so on. But theorizing and proving are two different things. And cops prefer proof.

The second problem was that I had no idea who he was.

But I had an idea where I might find him. In the same place I was thinking of looking for him when he was merely Brioche's alibi: at one of the burlesque shows he probably frequented. It wasn't a perfect plan, I admit. If I couldn't track him down, I'd be no better off than I was before I tagged him as a suspect. But at least now I had something to work with.

Brioche had been sitting quietly, scrutinizing my face as I worked through the idea. I stood up, thanked her for her time, and left her place eager to track down my new lead.

And, as an added bonus, I wasn't dead.

How about that, Filthy?

I told you so.

CHAPTER 12

Unfortunately, adding a suspect is a far cry from convicting a murderer, and there was still a triple-D bra full of information I didn't have. Like an answer to the question that had been bothering me from the moment I got LuLu's note the night of the show: Why the hell had she booked Victoria in the first place? (As Cherries said: Why would anyone?) If I knew that, I'd know…well, something. Maybe it would lead to a person other than LuLu who knew beforehand that Victoria was going to be performing that night. And that, I realized, would be useful. Because in order to premeditate murder, it helps to know that the victim is going to be in the location at which you premeditate killing her.

The only person who could answer these questions was the person who'd booked Victoria in the first place, and that was LuLu. I was tempted to try calling her again, but I decided not to—I didn't feel like another heartfelt conversation with her voicemail. Instead, I went to her website. I knew that tonight was the night she was due back in town, and the "Schedule" page on her site confirmed it. She would be hosting the midnight show at the Gilded Heel. I checked the time. Midnight was still several hours

away, but that was just as well. It would give me some
time to mull over what I'd learned so far.

But the street's no place for contemplation, and dry's
no way to do it. So I found a quiet bar with a late happy
hour, ordered a pint, and sat in a corner with my back
to the wall. Still being careful, as promised.

In my head, I went through my newly expanded
suspect list: the five performers who were in the show,
plus one creepy guy.

All six of them had opportunity, some more than
others. Unfortunately, the two with the most opportunity—the creepy guy, who'd spent a lot of time near
the alcove, and Angelina, who'd arrived early—were
the ones with the least evidence of motive. (Angelina
developed a motive pretty damn quick once the show
began, but that didn't mean she had a reason to paw
through Victoria's bag before.) Next up was Brioche.
She had lingered near the alcove with only the creepy
guy for company, and until I managed to track him
down there was no way of knowing how much of that
time she had spent chatting and how much she'd had
available for potentially more homicidal activities.
Then Eva—she might have emerged from the bathroom sooner than she had let on and taken a moment
to tamper with Victoria's bag before rushing backstage to tell the rest of us who she'd seen. Then
Jillian, who'd spent barely half a minute behind the
curtain with the bags, though that was probably just
enough time to switch a fake bottle of poison for a
real one. And coming in dead last in terms of opportunity was Cherries, because I had stashed her bag

for her. As far as motive went, I figured those last four were pretty much on equal footing, even if I'd need to learn Danish to decipher the exact nature of Brioche's complaint.

So how to narrow it down?

If LuLu had shared the fact that Victoria was going to be in the show with anyone, that would point pretty decisively in the direction of that person. But what if LuLu hadn't? What if no one else knew?

I took another sip of my beer. As I watched the bubbles float up from the bottom of the glass, a theory began bubbling up in my brain. By the time nothing remained of my drink but a thin layer of foam, that theory had become a full-fledged supposition, and one that sounded pretty damn good to me. It was pure conjecture, with no evidence to support it, but if true, it provided a more than satisfactory explanation for one aspect of the problem at hand.

It went something like this:

Let's say Victoria wasn't the only one to arrive early that night. Let's say the murderer—we'll call her 'M' for short—did too. Why? Plenty of possibilities: Maybe our Miss M is going out to dinner and wants to drop her bag in the alcove so she doesn't have to drag it to the restaurant. Maybe she's meeting a friend (Krash, for example) at Topkapi for a pre-show drink. Maybe she just feels like winding down at the bar before getting up on stage. Any of these explanations would do, and so would about a thousand others. Anyway, the why didn't matter, just the fact that she got there early.

As she approaches Topkapi, M sees Victoria walking

into the bar, dragging her bag. M asks herself: "What the hell? Why is *she* here—and why does she have a gig bag with her?" Rather than confronting Victoria, M watches through the window, staying out of sight. She sees Victoria go into the bar. Sees Victoria talking to Casey. Sees Casey point her towards the alcove. Sees Victoria go behind the curtains with her bag and emerge without it.

"I wonder," M thinks, "what exactly that bag contains. Is it perhaps an act Victoria has stolen? If only there were some way I could look inside…" As it turns out, M gets the chance to do just that, because the next thing she sees is Victoria leaving the bar. M hides herself in a doorway until Victoria is out of sight, waits until the bartender's back is turned, and sneaks through the bar to take a quick peek in the alcove. When she opens Victoria's suitcase, she finds a gothic black dress —so far, not terribly suspicious. Lots of performers have similar dresses. But when M digs further, she finds the black rose and the bottle marked POISON. She recognizes the props from Angelina's act, either because she has seen Angelina do the number or because she is Angelina. Either way, she's furious. Maybe she considers stealing the props, or even the whole suitcase, to sabotage the act, but then it occurs to her that there might be a way to put the kibosh on more than just this one incident. Maybe there's a way to prevent Victoria from stealing acts…permanently.

M knows that the number Angelina performs using these props includes a bit where she drinks from the bottle of poison. And if Angelina does it, it's a pretty good bet that the plagiarist will do it too. After all, that's what Victoria does, copies other people's acts, move for move, beat for beat, bump for bump, twirl for twirl.

But what if the bottle actually contained what it says it contains? What if, instead of whatever harmless beverage she filled it with originally, Victoria found herself pouring actual poison into her mouth while in the process of stealing the act? It would be poetic justice, something that might appeal to any of the five women in the Dreamland show that night.

So M rushes off to one of the local bodegas and purchases an identical bottle of Pest-Aside Liquid Rat poison. And when she gets back to Topkapi, she switches it for the prop.

It was simple, it was feasible, and it was a scenario that could easily apply to any of the women in the show. But in order for the theory to work, I needed to know two things for sure: that it had definitely been Victoria's bag in the alcove with Angelina's when I arrived (I had been assuming it was, but in a court of law my assumptions would carry about as much weight as a diva with back problems) and, if the bag was indeed Victoria's, that she had dropped it off herself. (If someone else had delivered her suitcase to Topkapi for her, that meant I had another brand-new suspect to consider.)

There was one person I could think of who probably knew the answer to both questions.

*

I stepped up to the velvet rope. The big guy behind it moved his eyes. Barely. Just enough to get me into his peripheral vision. He blinked, judgmentally. Can a blink be judgmental? From a New York City club bouncer, absolutely. A streetlight buzzed above me.

"I'm a friend of Casey's," I said.

He blinked.

"Casey, the DJ," I explained. "DJ Casey?"

In addition to running the sound and lights for Dreamland Burlesque and the comedy show preceding, Casey picked up DJ gigs at dance clubs around the city, his specialty being parties with a 1980s theme. I'm not talking mainstream 80s—Casey was fully alterno, several notches left of the dial, and just a few decades too late. When at these parties, he always wore the same blue leather jacket with squared shoulders, and you could be certain that at least one of his eyes would be covered by his bangs at all times.

"Casey," I repeated. "He's DJ'ing tonight."

The streetlight flickered overhead. This club, like so many of its kind, was in a defunct warehouse on a run-down industrial block—no residents means fewer noise complaints. The music pumping out of the doors right now was shaking the glass on a car parked across the street.

The bouncer blinked again, then broke into a wide smile.

"I'm just messing with you," he said. "Don't you recognize me, Porkpie? It's Roc. I used to do the door over at the Ukraine."

"Roc? You look different in a suit. Where's your hair?"

"Shaved it off. Better bald than balding, you know? Good to see you, though, dude, good to see you. Go on in. Hey, Stevey, that's Jonny Porkpie, he's okay, let him through."

The guy in the ticket booth waved me by and I walked into a wall of flashing lights and a barely recognizable techno 80s remix blasted at a volume far in excess of comfort or comprehension. The DJ booth, to my dismay, was all the way on the other side of the dance floor. I squeezed into the crowd, which throbbed vaguely to the music. The place was packed ass to elbows, and making my way across it required a delicate balance of dexterity, politeness, and good old-fashioned shoving.

Finally, I arrived at the DJ booth. I knocked on the plexiglas. Casey was wearing headphones and didn't hear me, so I made my way around till I was standing in front of him and waved. Vigorously.

He waved back, held up one finger, changed the record, then leaned over the booth to shake my hand.

"Oh, um, hey—Mr. Mayor!" he said.

"Hi," I shouted.

"Is Filthy with you?"

"No, I'm here alone."

"What?" Casey put a hand to his ear.

"I said," I yelled, "I'm alone!"

"Well…'hi' to…for me."

"What?"

"Say 'hi' to Filthy."

"Sure. Hey, can I ask you some questions about the night that girl died?" I said.

"What?"

"I said, can I ask you some questions about the night that girl died?"

"Oh…that." He shook his head. "That really kinda…"

"What?"

"That really sucked!"

"Right. Can I ask you some questions about it?" I yelled.

"What?" He cupped a hand to his ear.

(And like that. For the purposes of moving the things along, and my own sanity, I'll cut all the "what"s and repetitions from the rest of our conversation.)

"Can I ask you a few questions about Wednesday?" I repeated.

"Oh, um, yeah, sure."

"Victoria—the girl who died?"

"Oh. Her."

"When did you first meet her?"

"That night."

"You never saw her before Wednesday?"

"No."

"Ever hear anyone talk about her?"

"No, um, I don't think so. Not that I remember, anyway."

"So the first time you met her was when I saw you talking to her? When she told you to play her music loud?"

"No, I met her earlier. But it was that night. She got there before the comedy show—"

"She did?" I couldn't quite hide my excitement. "When?"

"I don't know. Pretty soon after the bar opened. Seven? Seven-thirty?"

"What did she do when she got there?"

"She tried to go backstage, and when I told her 'not yet' she was, um, annoyed, I guess. I said she could put her bag in the alcove, and she did, and then left."

Excellent. So far, my theory was solid. And if Casey saw someone else arrive at Topkapi before I got there, I might just have my murderer.

"What about the other performers?" I said. "Did any of them come in around the same time as Victoria?"

"I didn't see anyone, but I was mostly in the back setting up for the comedy show."

"How about a guy in an overcoat, with a big bushy beard?"

"What about him?"

"Did you see him? He spent a lot of time by the curtains."

Casey shrugged and shook his head. "Oh, um, sorry," he said. "Don't remember him. Hold on." He turned back to the board and cross-faded the song that was ending into another song that sounded nearly identical.

I suppose it had been too much to hope that Casey would solve the whole thing for me. But—with the exception of my eardrums—I was still in better shape than I had been when I walked in. I thanked Casey and made my way back through the throng.

As I hit the sidewalk it struck me that I should probably add Casey to my suspect list. But it would only be

for completeness—I didn't think there was a chance in
hell he had actually done it. Other than the Dreamland show, he had no connection to burlesque, and he
really seemed to have no idea who Victoria was, or
what she had done, other than die onstage. Of course
she had treated him like crap the night of the show,
but…it certainly wasn't the first time a performer had
given him a hard time, and he was a little too laid back
to be driven to murder by that sort of thing.

I headed back to the East Village. There was one
more piece of my theory that needed a plausibility
check. And there was still some time left before LuLu
would be done with the show at the Gilded Heel.

There are no fewer than eleven bodegas, delis, mar-
kets, groceries, and convenience stores within a five-
minute walk of Topkapi. Expand that to a ten-minute
walk and the number triples. Which means that there
were plenty of places that a would-be murderer, after
discovering what was in Victoria's bag, might go to
look for a bottle of Pest-Aside Liquid Rat Poison.

But would she be able to find one?

I started at Topkapi and worked my way out. The
first dozen places I stopped into didn't stock anything
of the sort. I quit asking at the counter after a few tries
because it occurred to me a guy who tried to buy rat
poison at every store on First through Third Avenues
might attract some negative attention. So I scoured
the aisles myself. No luck.

It was at the thirteenth stop that I hit the jackpot.
Tucked into the back corner of a run-down bodega,

between roach traps and boxes of stale pasta, sat a single lonely bottle of Pest-Aside. I picked it up. It wasn't much, one bottle in thirteen stores, but it was enough to confirm that my theory was plausible.

I looked up to find the cashier staring at me. I smiled at him. I held up the bottle and asked, "Good for rats?"

He grunted and shrugged, which was probably an appropriate response to such an inane question. But now I had called attention to the bottle. Could I put it back down and walk out? No…my least suspicious course of action was probably to buy the damn thing.

"That all?" the cashier said when I brought it to the counter. I nodded, and he rang me up.

As I gave him the cash, I considered asking the guy if any burlesque performers or men in overcoats had also bought a bottle of the stuff in the last few days, but I thought better of it. It didn't seem like a good idea for a murder suspect buying a bottle of poison to make more of a spectacle of himself, especially when he was purchasing the same product that had put a woman in the morgue just two nights ago. The guy was already watching me suspiciously. So I took my change and headed outside.

When I hit the sidewalk, I realized that poison was also not the smartest thing for a murder suspect to be carrying around. So I tossed the bottle in the trash and glanced at my watch. The bodega crawl had taken more time than I'd intended, and LuLu's show would be almost over by now. If I wanted to catch her before she left, I was going to have to shake a leg. I stepped out into the street, hailed a cab, and told him to step on it.

CHAPTER 13

LuLu LaRue had developed a bunch of different hosting personalities over the years. As producer and host of a weekly show, it was one way she kept her regulars coming back for more. Sometimes she was a stern German nurse, sometimes a vintage movie star, *dah-ling*, sometimes a deep-voiced butch with a guitar who sang raunchy lesbian folk songs. The character she was playing when I walked in the door of the Gilded Heel was, I have to admit, my least favorite of her personae—an over-the-hill borscht-belt comedian named Allan Schmuck, with a wide black moustache, a penchant for Yiddish, and a repertoire of jokes straight out of a Catskills reject pile. She did the character well, don't get me wrong—sold it completely, and audiences were buying, but I still thought it was a bargain basement routine from such a talented woman. The accent was a bit too thick and the humor a bit too broad—and coming from me, that's saying something. The schtick worked best with a drummer to back her up, putting stings after her clunkers to let the audience know when to laugh, but tonight she was working solo.

"…just back in the dressing room mit the goils. I try to give every goil a kiss on each cheek before she goes on stage… If there's enough time, sometimes I make it all the way up to her face! Oy!"

Oy, indeed. LuLu finished the set, bringing all the performers on stage for a final bow, and bid the audience a fond farewell (and, somewhat embarrassingly, but in keeping with the character, a "good yontif") as the curtains closed.

I found a stool at the bar—the whiskey was there waiting for me almost before I sat down—and waited for LuLu to emerge. But she didn't. All of the other performers in the show did, one after another, dragging their gig bags behind them. But no LuLu. Had she slipped out the side door when I wasn't looking? I didn't think so—I'd been keeping my eyes open.

I polished off my drink and slipped through the gap in the curtains, thinking I'd find LuLu in the dressing room. I was wrong. There she was, sitting in a chair on the stage. She was still wearing the full Allan Schmuck drag, which was strange—I knew from past complaints that the getup could get pretty uncomfortable after a long night, and that she usually liked to get out of it as quickly as possible after the show ended.

She had her head in her hands. I touched her shoulder, and she looked up.

"So you heard what happened?" I said.

"Yeah." She dragged herself to her feet. "I swear, Porkpie, I leave the show with you for one night…" She shook her fist in the air melodramatically.

"Hey, you're the one who told me to knock 'em dead," I said.

Neither of us laughed, probably because it wasn't funny. LuLu stepped off the stage and into the dressing room. She took a makeup wipe from a package on the counter and rubbed the moustache off her upper lip.

"You got my messages, then?" I said.

LuLu folded the makeup wipe to expose the clean side and used it to remove the remaining smears of black from her face. "Oh, no, I—my phone's been dead for a few days. Forgot to bring my charger with me on my trip." She pointed to the wall outlet, where the phone in question was plugged in. She started unbuttoning Allan Schmuck's pink frilly tux shirt.

"So you found out—"

"When I walked in here tonight." She took off the shirt, folded it, and put it in her suitcase. "Just had time when I got back to pick up my costume and charger at home before heading here. The bartender thought I knew, made some comment. I asked him what he meant. Had to sit down for a few minutes."

"I bet," I said. "I'm sorry."

"Not your fault, Porkpie," she said. "Unless you killed her. Rumor has it that's what the cops think." She unwrapped the ace bandage she used to flatten her chest when playing Allan and dropped it in her suitcase. Then she took it out again, rolled it into a tight wad, and tucked it back in. She massaged her breasts. A couple of hours strapped down left them pretty sore. After my experience at Jillian's dungeon earlier today, I could sympathize. "Did you kill her, Porkpie?"

"No, I didn't," I said. "But yes, that's what the cops think. So, because I'm fairly fond of not being in jail, I'm trying to find out who did."

"Well, if I can help in any way…"

"Yeah," I said. "You can. By telling me something: Why did you book her, LuLu?"

She chuckled. It was a dry, humorless sound. "I guess…it seemed like a good idea at the time?"

"Seriously, Lu. What were you doing? I know you—you're not the type of person who would book someone like that just to get a reciprocal gig."

"No, no. Of course not. I would never do her show, are you kidding?" She pulled off her pants, held them by the cuffs, crease to crease, folded them neatly, and tossed them on top of the rest of the clothes in her bag.

"So, what—did you lose a bet?"

"Look, I was…I wanted to…" She took a deep breath. "It was to teach her a lesson."

"A lesson?"

"Right. Sort of a, I guess, an object lesson. Put her in a show with a bunch of people she'd screwed over. Maybe when she found herself in a dressing room where everyone hated her, she'd see, I don't know, the consequences of her actions. The error of her ways. Some idiot thing like that. Turned out to be not such a hot idea, obviously."

"But why her? I mean, I know why *her*, there's plenty of reasons someone might want to set her up like that. But why you? I don't remember you mentioning that she ever did anything to you."

"She didn't. Not directly. A lot of my friends. You. But not me."

"So what made you decide it was your job to teach her a lesson?"

She slipped her arms into a bra, and reached around

behind her back to hook it. She adjusted her breasts in the cups, then picked up a t-shirt. "It just sort of happened, really. She emailed me a couple months ago out of the blue, saying she was going to be in town this week and asking for a booking at Dreamland. As if I didn't know about the things she'd done to my friends. I thought it was good for a chuckle and a quick delete, but the friend I was hanging out with had a different idea: a show called 'Just Desserts.' It would star Jillian and Filthy and Eva and as many other people as we could cram in that Victoria had screwed over... and Victoria herself would be the very special guest."

"If that was the concept, why include Angelina? She didn't have any problem with Victoria—at least, not until that night."

"Angelina..." LuLu pulled the t-shirt over her head with a sigh. "She was booked for that night long before we ever came up with the idea. I asked her to switch dates, but she refused. I don't know if you've seen how she gets—"

"I've seen how she gets."

"Right. So I figured, what the hell. One wildcard won't matter."

"I see. And why didn't you at least let the rest of us in on the scheme?"

"I don't know. Loose lips, and all that, I guess. The fewer people know, the less chance it gets back to Victoria." She shook her head. "Don't look at me like that, Jonny."

"Who was the friend?"

"What?"

"The friend you were hanging out with. The one who suggested 'Just Desserts' in the first place." I had a sneaking suspicion I knew who it was—I could smell that particular acerbic sense of humor from a mile away, but I hoped I was wrong. I desperately wanted to be wrong.

"I don't want to get anyone in trouble."

"If she's the murderer, she's already in trouble."

"I don't think she'd do anything like that."

"Who was it?"

"I really don't—" She ran a hand through her hair and pulled at the bottom of her t-shirt.

"Lu, come on. This isn't a game. We're talking about difference between the police arresting a killer and the police arresting me."

"Jonny—"

"*Who?*"

LuLu took a deep breath.

"Cherries." She said.

Cherries.

I was right.

Damn.

And after all that crap she'd been giving me back-stage. "Why the hell would LuLu book her?" she'd said. My ass. She'd strung me along like a pink feather boa in a sixteen-minute striptease, amused herself by accusing me of the very thing she was doing: with-holding knowledge of the fact that Victoria was in the show that night.

Damn it, Cherries was my friend. If she was a murderer, too, I'd kill her.

"Just because the show was her idea, that doesn't necessarily mean she killed Victoria," LuLu said.

"Right," I said. "Sure." I turned and walked out of the dressing room, across the stage and out through the curtains, past the chairs and to the bar. LuLu followed me. I ordered a round. We drank for a few minutes in silence.

"Hey," LuLu said, finally. "This is going to sound terrible, and I'm not saying I believe that Cherries would—you know. But if she did, I mean, you know, well…am I an accessory to murder?"

I shrugged. I didn't have much else left in me. LuLu bit her lip, finished her drink, said goodbye, and went backstage to get her stuff.

It was late. Very late. But I wasn't ready to head home yet.

CHAPTER 14

So, here's how I ended up in the Hindenburg.

I was at the bar. I was drinking another whiskey—a double—with a whiskey back, a whiskey on the side, and a whiskey chaser.

I was thinking of ordering a whiskey.

The Gilded Heel was closed for the night, but they sometimes let performers hang around after the doors are locked, until the staff is ready to go home.

Liquid courage, some call it, the brown stuff in my hand. But it wasn't doing me a whole hell of a lot of good. It's one thing to accuse a friend of murder in a general sense, as one of a group of potential suspects. But it's quite another to actually have proof. I had proof. And I'm not just talking about the 80-proof in my glass.

I thought it over. I wanted to be sure. I wanted to be *very* sure.

I was pretty sure. Unless she was lying, and I didn't see any reason why she would be, LuLu's revelation had shoved Cherries right up to the top of the suspect list. But pretty sure wasn't sure enough, not when it could lead to one of us spending the rest of our life in prison.

I took a sip. The more I thought about it, the more things pointed in Cherries' direction. She certainly had motive enough, and as for opportunity—well, if she had shown up early and tampered with the bottle, it wasn't hard to imagine her deliberately staging an overblown, hands-full arrival later, to get me to stow her bag for her in order to shield herself from suspicion. Just on a performance level, it was the sort of thing she would have enjoyed.

Then there was the thing she said right before Victoria dropped dead.

"And then she dies."

At the time, it just seemed like a description of what would happen next in the act. She'd seen Angelina do the original, after all. But like I said, I knew Cherries' sense of humor pretty well. She loved making oblique remarks that only people in the know would understand. In this case, she would have been the only audience for her own wit, but that had never stopped her before.

But would she go as far as to kill someone? Even someone she hated? I didn't want to think so. But finding out that someone plagiarized one of your acts—especially one of your best acts—was the artistic equivalent of a punch in the gut. I knew from experience. And Cherries had a temper; the woman held a grudge tighter than an undersized g-string. Who knows what might drive someone completely over the edge?

I took another sip. I was taking my time with the drink, putting off for as long as I could the moment when I'd have to leave the comfort of the Gilded Heel, step out into the warm, dark night and…do what? Tell the cops what I had learned? Go home? Confront Cherries?

Then came the tapping on the front door. The bartender finished wiping the glass in his hand, put it on the rack above his head, and walked around the bar. He pulled the shade on the front door back an inch to peek outside. When he did, I saw a glint of streetlight reflected on something metal. He unlocked the door and opened it a crack—which was strange. They never let people into the Gilded Heel after closing time, not even performers. If you were in, you were in. If you were out, you stayed out. Unless…

Unless the flash of metal had been a badge.

Because a cop was one of the few people for whom the doors would be opened after hours.

I told myself I was being paranoid. It was 4:30 in the morning. This was probably the night porter, just getting to work. What would the police be doing here at this hour? And even if it were the NYPD, there were a thousand reasons they might be knocking on the door that had nothing to do with me.

Then I remembered the bodega. If the clerk had decided to be a good citizen and call his local precinct to report that a long-haired, hat-wearing man had behaved in a suspicious manner while purchasing a bottle of Pest-Aside Liquid Rat Poison, and word had filtered through the building until it reached the desks of Officers Brooklyn and Bronx…

When your top suspect in a murder by poison buys another bottle of the stuff, you might decide that it's time to hit the local burlesque haunts and try to track him down, see if you can figure out what he's doing with it sooner rather than later.

But no, I told myself again, I was just being paranoid. And I kept telling myself that until I heard the voice.

There was no mistaking that voice. Even through the door and across the room, the accent came across clearly. If it wasn't Officer Brooklyn, he had a twin brother who was also on the force. And if the voice wasn't enough to convince me I was in trouble, what it was saying did.

"...looking for a performer," the voice said. "Name of Jonny Pork—"

I hopped off my stool and headed towards the back of the room. Before Officer Brooklyn had finished his sentence, the emergency exit door was closing behind me.

Twenty minutes later, I looked up at Cherries's window and tried to picture how the big denouement was going to play out. My stern accusation, her tearful confession (well, probably not tearful—Cherries wasn't the crying type), her flirtatious attempt to convince me to keep my mouth shut, my firm and cold insistence on justice, and then perhaps a short bout of attempted murder to prevent me from revealing her secret. What better way to end a Friday night?

I rang the bell.

"Yeah?" her voice sounded tense, even through the intercom. She hadn't been asleep, I can tell you that.

"Porkpie," I said. The lock clicked, and I pushed the door open. I still had five flights ahead of me before I could accuse my friend of homicide. I took the stairs slowly.

Not just because my knees hurt, either.

Cherries' apartment wasn't locked. I walked in, leaving the door open behind me, which is never done in New York City (except, of course, in sitcoms written by those L.A. writers from Ohio). But I figured, since I was probably no safer inside than out, why not leave myself an unobstructed escape route?

The room was dark. The streetlight threw a dramatic glow through the window, casting sharp and ominous shadows over the clutter of Cherries Jubilee's living room. The light streaming in from the hallway behind me revealed the star of the scene slumped on her couch wearing nothing but a button-down shirt and a pair of boys' Y-fronts. The shirt, fastened with a single button, barely covered her body from her neck to her thighs.

"So," she said when she saw the expression on my face, "you found out."

"Yeah," I said. "I found out."

"I didn't lie to you," she said, pointing one finger at my chest.

"What?"

"I was very careful not to lie to you. I mean, crime of omission, sure, but I never flat-out *lied*."

"You never *lied* to me?"

"Never."

"Does that matter, Cherries?"

"Look, I know you're mad at me, and I'm really sorry—"

"*Mad* at you? You're *sorry?* Are you insane? I mean, of course you're insane, you killed someone, but…"

"I did what?"

"Killed someone."

"Bullshit."

"Oh, come on. You had a grudge against Victoria— justified, absolutely, but still a grudge, so you set up the revenge show with LuLu—"

"What? The show was her idea!"

"That's not what she says. And anyway, who are you talking to? I know you. You're a born instigator. You got LuLu to book the rest of us in that show to spread the suspicion around among five equally angry suspects. Or maybe you didn't even plan to kill her originally, but when you looked in her bag and saw that she was still stealing numbers, you lost it…"

I ran Cherries through the rest of the scenario. I told her about Victoria arriving early with her bag, about the poison available at the nearby bodega. I enumerated the things that pointed her direction, like the comments she had made at the show that no longer seemed innocent. When I was done talking, Cherries stood up.

She walked towards me. I stood my ground. It was clear she wasn't hiding any weapons in that outfit.

Cherries stepped around me and closed her front door. I heard a lock being locked, then another, and the rattle of a chain.

She strolled over to her kitchen. As she walked, I

couldn't help noticing the bottom of the shirt sneaking up to reveal her…but no—this woman was a killer. An incredibly sexy killer, but a killer nonetheless. She opened a drawer and I heard the rattle of cutlery.

Call me crazy, but it sounded like knives. I don't know if knives have a different tone than other silverware, but to me, at that moment, it sounded like knives.

I glanced at the front door. With three pieces of hardware to navigate in order to unlock it, it would take longer for me to open than it would for her to stab me to death. The door to her bedroom was closed, as was the door to her bathroom. So my quickest egress was the nearest window. But it was only open a crack. Could I get to it and squeeze through before she could reach me?

Cherries turned to face me. Something glinted in her hand.

She took a step in my direction.

Then turned to her fridge, opened it, and took out a beer. She used the bottle opener she was holding to pry the cap off, then put it back in the silverware drawer. She brushed against me as she walked by again on her way to the couch. She sat down and crossed her legs.

She took a long swig of the beer, keeping her eyes on me the whole time. She wiped a bit of foam off her lip. "So," she said. "Just to clarify, in order for your little theory to work, I would need to have been in and out of Topkapi long before the time you saw me arrive, is that right?"

"Yes," I said.

"So if I were somewhere else during all that time, would that eliminate me from consideration?"

"If you could prove it, I guess."

"Here's the thing, Porkpie. From about six o'clock until about ten minutes before you saw me walk in the door, I was having dinner with a friend."

"Oh, yeah?" I said. "Who?"

She looked at me.

There was a mischievous twinkle in her eye that was wholly inappropriate given the circumstances.

"Your wife," she said.

Ah.

An alibi.

Cherries had an alibi. I hadn't been thinking along those lines. But she was right: my theory required the murderer to arrive at Topkapi initially sometime between seven P.M., when the bar opened, and when I arrived at nine. So anyone who had an alibi for the two hours before the show was out of the running. And Cherries had just presented a doozy of a witness.

"If you don't believe me, call her. Or are you worried she'll be mad if you wake her up?" Cherries said, taking another sip of her beer.

So I called her.

"Did I wake you?" I said, when Filthy picked up the phone.

"No, actually," Filthy said. "Couldn't sleep. Just sitting here watching TV, wondering if you'd gotten yourself killed yet. Have you gotten yourself killed yet? Where are you?"

"Back at Cherries'," I said.

"This is some torrid affair you two are having."

"You should see what she's wearing."

"Keep it up, I'll get jealous. Not of her, of you."

"I need to ask you something. Before you went to the Gilded Heel on Wednesday, what were you doing?"

"Same thing you're doing now," she said. "Cherries."

"Seriously."

"Seriously? She and I were having dinner."

"Where?"

"That obnoxious pizza place on First."

"Do you remember when she left the restaurant?"

"Same as I did—in time to get to our respective gigs."

"And she was with you from six o'clock until then?"

"Yes, we met at the— Who's the ringing the damn doorbell at this time of night? Hold on. Yes? Who is it—oh. I'll call you back." Filthy hung up.

Cherries leaned back on the sofa and played with the button of her shirt. Her eyes were fixed on mine. She was trying very hard to suppress a smirk.

I put my phone back in my pocket.

She snapped the elastic on her underwear and took a sip of her beer.

I lifted my hat and scratched my head.

She cleared her throat.

I put my hat back on.

Cherries sighed. "So?" she said.

"Yeah," I said.

"Yeah, what?" she said.

"She said…yeah."

"Uh-huh."

"So...yeah." I said.

"Am I now cleared of all charges by the Porkpie P.D.?"

"For the time being." Until I could think of an alternate theory that didn't require her to be in two places at once. But at the moment, I couldn't.

"Uh-huh," she said. "Is there, maybe, anything else you want to say? To me? Maybe? You think?"

"I...ah... Did you tell anyone else that Victoria was going to be in the show that night?"

"Really? Out of all the things you could have chosen, that's what you decided to say?"

"There's still a murderer running around," I said.

"Who *isn't* me. Agreed?"

"As far as I can tell."

"Jackass," Cherries said, and polished off her beer. She rolled off the couch and headed to the kitchen for another. "Fine. What was your question?"

"Who else knew that Victoria was going to be there?"

"Other than LuLu and me? No one." The beer fizzed over when she opened it. The cap rattled when it hit the sink. Cherries slurped at the spillage.

"You didn't drop any hints?"

"Yes, fine, I dropped a couple hints."

"Did anyone pick up on one of those hints, you think?"

"Oh, I really don't think so."

"Because Jillian mentioned..."

"I'm sure they were obvious in hindsight," Cherries said, sitting back down.

I joined her on the couch next to her and massaged my temples. Look, I didn't want Cherries to be the murderer. And if—as now seemed to be the case—she wasn't, that was fantastic. I liked Cherries, especially in that shirt. Even if she had set the whole ill-fated evening in motion with her suggestion to LuLu, at least she wasn't a psychotic killer.

But none of this was good news for a guy who had just ducked out on a couple of police officers. When I believed I was running away in order to deliver them the real murderer, that had seemed like a relatively bright idea. It didn't seem like such a bright idea now. What could I tell them? What information had I gathered by running away? That I had almost definitely eliminated one suspect? Whom they had never suspected?

"You really thought I killed her?" Cherries was now more bemused than angry. "And you came all the way to my apartment to confront me? Unarmed? Alone? In the middle of the night? A murderous murdering murderer like me? Priceless. You're priceless, Jonny. And pretty damn ballsy, too. I'm impressed."

I shrugged.

"Oh, Jonny. You need a drink."

"I've had a few."

"Have another," she said, and got up to pour me a whiskey. It was slightly better than my usual brand, but I drank it anyway. "You still think the cops are trying to hang this on you, huh?"

"They didn't track me down at The Gilded Heel to buy me a drink."

"The police tracked you…?"

My phone rang. It was Filthy again.

"You'll never guess who that was at the door," she said.

"Your boyfriend?" I said. "Your girlfriend? My boyfriend?"

"Close. Couple of policemen with completely improbable accents. They wanted to invite you over to their place for a little chat, but apparently they couldn't seem to track you down. Requested in the most emphatic terms that I give them a buzz if I heard from you. And furthermore, get this, I peeked out the window a minute ago, and you'll never guess who's across the street. Give up? It's…somebody! Just standing there, hanging out on the corner in the middle of the night for no particular reason, but with a great view of our front door.

"Drug dealer? Not quite the type. Mugger? Little bit too clean-cut. Cop on stakeout? Ding ding ding ding ding. Thought you might like to know, in case you wanted to make other sleeping arrangements. Don't do anyone I wouldn't do!"

"Thanks," I said. "Try to get some sleep."

"Oh, yeah, sure, absolutely," Filthy said, and hung up.

I put my phone back in my pocket and looked up at my host.

"So…" I said. "This might be a strange question, after all that's just happened…"

"Yeah?" Cherries said. That twinkle was back in her eye.

"Can I crash here?"

"Here?"

"Yeah."

"Does Filthy need privacy? Using your place for an assignation?"

"Something like that. She's got a thing for cops on stakeout, and there seems to be one hanging out across the street from our apartment."

"Kinky."

"So, can I stay?"

Cherries grinned. Oh, that grin.

"You're *that* sure I'm not the murderer?" She said.

"At this point, Cherries, I'm so exhausted I don't give a rat's ass."

Another couple of whiskeys later, as the first rays of sunlight stretched over the borough of Queens, I was curled up on Cherries' couch and trying to sleep.

It wasn't going well. My mind was racing. The cops were so interested in talking to me that they were staking out my house. And even if I stayed away from the apartment, in this city, I couldn't avoid the cops forever.

I was running out of time.

CHAPTER 15
SATURDAY

I woke up to Cherries' buzzer.

Buzzing.

And buzzing.

Cherries emerged from her bedroom rubbing her eyes. She had on what she called pajamas. Cherries doesn't wear a lot to bed.

I was pleased to discover that I'd woken up alive. It was further evidence of my friend's innocence.

"What the hell?" she said. "What time—who the hell would ring my bell at the ungodly hour of eleven A.M.?" She pressed the buzzer. "Yeah. Who is it?"

"Police, ma'am," said a voice that, though muffled through the intercom, clearly belonged to Officer Bronx.

Cherries released the intercom button and looked over at me. "You didn't share your little theory about me with anyone else, did you?"

"No." I sat up on the couch. "I wanted to talk to you first."

"So what the hell are the cops doing here?"

"You're asking me? I'm the one who slept on your couch because they were staking out my house."

"Do I let them in?"

"Do they sound like they know I'm here?"

"*Do they sound like—*? Yeah, Jonny, those two words she said had a definite Porkpie-awareness about them."

The buzzer rang again.

"I think I have to let them in," she said. "You—I don't know—go out the window. Hold on a minute, sorry." That last was into the intercom. She jerked a thumb towards the window. "That one's got the fire escape."

"I want to hear what they ask you. I'll hide in the closet."

"Oh, that's clever. That's really clever. The closet. They'll never think to look there. Plus, Jonny, have you *seen* my closets?"

"So, where? Under the couch? In the shower?"

Cherries pointed to the thing that was taking up much of one corner of her living room.

"Hindenburg," she said. I mentioned earlier that Cherries owns a wearable replica of the Hindenburg, right?

There was a hole in the bottom of the costume out of which Cherries' legs protruded when she was performing her Hindenburg number. The outfit had been custom made for Cherries, so it was a tight fit squeezing my shoulders in, but once I had cleared the leghole and pulled my entire body inside, I was able to stretch out. A blimp costume has, by its very nature, plenty of extra room to it. I had an obscured but somewhat useful view of the room through one of the armholes.

Cherries went over to the intercom and buzzed the officers in.

Then she went to slip into something less revealing.

As much time passed as it takes for two police officers to heave themselves up five flights of stairs.

It felt like a lot longer.

There was a knock on the door.

I was breathing much louder than usual. At least, that's how it seemed. Maybe it was the shape of the costume that was amplifying my respirations. If I kept inhaling and exhaling at this volume, I was sure the detectives would hear me the moment they walked in, extract me from the zeppelin, and arrest me. I held my breath, but that didn't last long, and the subsequent exhalation was even louder. Okay, I figured, I'll breathe slowly instead. I tried it. I sounded like an obscene phone call.

Cherries emerged from her bedroom and opened the apartment door to reveal the two detectives.

"Somethin' wrong with your bell?" Officer Brooklyn asked.

"Took you a long time to buzz us in," observed Officer Bronx.

"A *very* long time," added Officer Brooklyn.

"Sorry, officers," Cherries said. "But when you rang my bell, I wasn't wearing *a thing*."

"Ah," said Officer Brooklyn.

"We won't take up much of your time, ma'am," said Officer Bronx.

"Not much at all," said Officer Brooklyn.

"Just a couple minutes," said Officer Bronx.

"You're friends with a Mr. Jonny Porkpie, right?" said Officer Brooklyn.

"Happen to see him at any time in the last twelve hours?" said Officer Bronx.

"Or had any contact with him whatsoever?" said Officer Brooklyn.

Cherries considered the question. "Oh, gosh, I don't know, officers. Last I saw Porkpie, ummmmm…" Oh, great. Cherries had decided to put on her dumb blonde act for the cops. "His plans were, uh, up in the air."

Oh, Cherries. She hadn't been considering the question, she'd been considering the gag.

If she kept sending them subliminal messages like that, one of the detectives was sure to glance in the blimp's direction sooner or later. I double-checked myself to make sure I hadn't accidentally left a shoelace or something like that sticking out any of the armholes, legholes, or head hole. I seemed fairly well stashed. All my component parts were firmly and fully in the blimp, from the tips of my shoes to the hat on my…wait a minute.

There was no hat on my head.

I looked out the armhole, angling my head so I could see the couch on which I had slept.

And there it was, on the coffee table.

My porkpie.

For crying out loud, how many detective novels have I read in my life? And yet I go and do a dumb thing like leave clear and tangible evidence of my presence right out in the open where any Officer Tom, Detective Dick, or Plainclothes Harry will see it.

Luckily, not from the doorway in which they were currently standing—I had at least that much going for me. But all they needed to do was take one step into the apartment, and the hat's out of the bag.

There was no way I could get to it without giving myself away. I couldn't slip out of the costume without being seen, and I had a feeling that the officers would become slightly suspicious if an entire blimp stood up and walked across the room.

"Oh! Now I remember! I can be *so* silly sometimes! Jonny dropped in yesterday," Cherries was saying, "to ask me questions. I thought he was just full of hot air. Why do you want to know? Is he a flight risk?"

Damn it, Cherries. Stop cracking jokes for a second and look behind you...

Wait.

Maybe there was a way I could tell her.

I reached for my pocket, slowly, slowly, keeping my hand close to my body so as not to shake the blimp too much. In the cramped quarters, I didn't have a lot of room to maneuver, but I slipped two fingers in and managed to extract my phone.

Then—gently, gently—I brought the phone up to my face. Oh, look at that. How clever of me: the ringer was still on. Here I was worried about my feet sticking out when all it would take was one incoming phone call to blow the whole thing sky high. I turned the sound off and typed out a three letter text message to Cherries.

Her phone buzzed. Cherries ignored it.

Officer Brooklyn was wondering aloud if they might be allowed to step inside the apartment for a moment to ask their questions.

I sent the message again. Cherries' phone buzzed again. She ignored it again, and told the officer that she didn't see why not.

I sent the message a third time. The phone buzzed. Annoyed, she picked it up and glanced at the screen.

And saw my message. Three letters: "H-A-T."

Her brow furrowed for a moment, and then she got it. Her eyes widened.

She glanced toward the living room. And she saw it. Hat.

Cherries stepped in front of the officers before they could cross her threshold. "Um…wait. Do you have a—what do you call that thing?—a warrant?" Cherries said.

"What?" said Officer Bronx.

"To come into the apartment. They always say on the teevee that you have to have a warrant."

"We don't need a warrant," said Officer Brooklyn.

"We're just here to ask some questions, ma'am," said Officer Bronx.

"I don't know…the place is a mess, so, you know, I'm kind of embarrassed," Cherries said.

"Right." Officer Bronx wasn't buying it. She sounded suspicious, and why the hell shouldn't she? Cherries wasn't exactly selling it.

"I mean, if you just want to ask some questions, I'm more than happy to have you—" Cherries began, but was interrupted by a *riiiiipppp*.

The sound of cloth pulling apart. More specifically, the cloth of Cherries' shirt, which she had somehow managed to catch on the doorknob. From my hiding place, I could see only her naked back as the shirt dropped to the floor. But the expressions on the faces of the detectives as they were treated to a full-frontal view more than made up for what I was missing on the other side.

"Whoops," Cherries said.

Officer Bronx blinked. Officer Brooklyn licked his lips involuntarily.

"I guess I'd better go put something on," Cherries said, and slammed the door shut.

She ran to the couch, grabbed my hat, and stuffed it through the armhole of the Hindenburg, hissing the word *"Idiot!"* as she did. I uncrushed the porkpie and put it back on my head. Then she ran to her bedroom, and emerged pulling on a tank top that only mostly covered what she had just revealed to the cops. Cherries knew her business. Good burlesque performers are experts in sexual misdirection. If your interrogators are so busy looking at the outline of your nipples through your shirt, they're probably not going to spend quite as much time looking over the rest of the room as they might otherwise have done.

She threw open her door so energetically that one of her breasts nearly popped out of the armhole of the tank top. "Gee gosh, I'm *so* sorry, officers. That must have been really embarrassing for you," she said, tucking herself back in. "Come on in. I was just about to make breakfast—Bloody Mary, anyone?"

Officer Bronx walked into the apartment, giving Cherries a hard look as she did so. Maybe Cherries wasn't on my own suspect list anymore, but I got the feeling she had just moved up a place or two on Officer Bronx's. Officer Brooklyn was also examining Cherries closely, but I wouldn't describe the look on his face as suspicion. At any rate, neither of the cops were looking at the blimp, and that was the whole point.

"Nothing for you guys? Okay, then. Now what were we talking about?" Cherries said, and absentmindedly flicked her hair out of her face as she plopped down on the couch. By sitting there, she forced the officers to stand—if they wanted to face her as they asked their questions—with their backs to the Hindenburg. Clever Cherries. "Oh, right, sorry," she continued, "I'm *such* a blonde sometimes. You were asking about Jonny, right? He was here Thursday asking me a lot of questions, almost like *he* was the one investigating that terrible, awful thing that happened the other night. I don't know what he's so concerned about. If the *fine* officers of the NYPD are looking into it, I'm *sure* you'll solve the case."

Officer Bronx said, "What time did you arrive at the venue on Wednesday night?"

"Me? Why?"

"It might be important."

"I dunno…I had a drink or two before the show started. But I didn't look at a clock or anything. The show never starts on time, so why bother?"

"Who was there when you arrived?"

"Oh, my, let's see, well, the bartender, of course, and DJ Casey, I think, though I didn't really see him until later, and Jonny, if that's who you're asking about, and then a couple other people, let's see, who were they? Well..." Cherries rambled on, using as many words as she could to convey as little information as possible, until Officer Bronx cut her off.

"I understand that there's an alcove where performers stash their bags before going backstage. Is that correct?"

"Oh, yes. That comedy show runs on and on, I mean, I'm not sure why, no one likes it, but they're *always* getting out late and we have to wait in the bar, not that that's a bad thing, that's where the drinks are, still it would be nice to—"

I was glad the police were also asking questions about the bags and the alcove. It meant they had probably discovered that Victoria's suitcase had arrived at the venue before any of the other performers. If it came to a court case, that might introduce what some would call "reasonable doubt." Of course, the fact that I was currently hiding from the cops in a blimp costume might make that doubt seem slightly less reasonable, but at this point, I was willing to take whatever I could get.

"How many other bags were present in the alcove when you put yours there?"

"Oh, I didn't see. Jonny stashed my bag for me that night," Cherries replied.

"Hmph," Officer Bronx said. "And when did you first notice that..."

This went on for a while. Bronx sounded like she was trying to get Cherries to confess to a closer proximity to the alcove than she was currently admitting.

Cherries, in response, rambled on so much that by the end it wasn't clear whether or not she in fact knew what a bag was.

Eventually the questions petered out. Bronx wrapped the interview up by handing Cherries a business card and saying, "If you see or hear from Mr. Porkpie, you should call us immediately."

"Oh, of *course*, Officer. Of *course* I will."

Officer Bronx twitched her head at Brooklyn, who followed her out into the hallway. He'd been unusually quiet during this interview, and I could count the reasons why on one chest.

Cherries walked after them, and watched from the doorway until they started down the stairs.

When they were out of earshot, she shut the door and turned to the blimp.

"Oh, the humanity!" she said.

"Oh, shut up," I replied.

CHAPTER 16

"This is a very good disguise," Filthy said, as she sat down opposite me. I glanced around the café, a half-assed bistro in Greenwich Village. Not a lot of style to the place and not a lot of room, either—but it did have a few tables tucked into nooks and crannies, where I could hole up out of view of the street and do the right thing by a cup of coffee or eight.

"An excellent disguise," Filthy continued, "for a man on the run. Very subtle. The call goes out over the police radio: 'Be on the lookout for a suspect named Jonny Porkpie.' 'But how will we recognize him?' says our hapless officer. 'Oh, I don't know,' the radio replies, 'maybe look for the guy *wearing a porkpie hat*.' Brilliant."

I took off the hat. Honestly, I wear it so often, I had forgotten it was on my head.

"Here. You can change the rest, too." She tossed a bag across the table, knocking over my coffee cup. Luckily, it was empty, but the clatter caught the attention of the waiter, who started walking in our direction. I signaled for a refill, and he rolled his eyes. He was probably justified in doing so. I'd been sitting there for hours.

I opened the bag and glanced inside, where Filthy had crammed a half-dozen changes of socks and underwear, a pair of pants, and a couple of shirts.

"You think I'll be gone this long?" I said.

"*I was a fugitive,*" Filthy said, "*from Justice. Yeah, Justice. That dame had it in for me, I could tell, and you don't want to get on the bad side of a blindfolded chick with a sword. Don't get me wrong. Even though she was on my ass like a hot potato, I had it bad for that babe—how can you not like a gal who strolls around town with one boob flapping in the breeze? But—*"

I interrupted her. "Really? Now? Now seems like a good time for that?"

"Why not? Hey, maybe I should do a Lady Justice number. Nah, it's probably been done. Maybe I'll just walk around with one boob hanging out."

"Seriously, though, Filthy—"

"So now, honey, tell me. Why are the nice police stalking you? And me? I had just a bitch of a time shaking the guy who was tailing me. I had to pull a reverse Hammett with a half-Houdini and a Cincinnati twist."

"You're making that up."

"I *am* making that up. Actually, I just jumped on the F train as the doors were closing. Who would have thought it would be so easy?" Filthy waited while the waiter refilled my cup. When he left she said, "So tell me, darling, what exactly have you been up to since… oh, was it only yesterday?"

I outlined, in as little detail as possible, my activities since she had last seen me, limping out of Jillian's dungeon. As I told the story, Filthy's expression changed from amused to annoyed. By the time I got into the Hindenburg, she was clutching her head in her hands.

"I knew I shouldn't have let you out of those shackles," she interjected as I was describing Cherries' cop-distracting tactics. She must genuinely have been worried. Under normal circumstances, she would never interrupt a story that involved one of her friends taking off her shirt.

"And you actually bought a bottle of the exact same poison that killed Victoria?"

I shrugged. Filthy shook her head.

"So let me guess what happened next," she said. "After Cherries flashed the cops and they left, you snuck out of Cherries' building—"

"I didn't *sneak* out of Cherries' building," I said. "I *escaped* from her building despite a veritable phalanx of police surveillance. It was pretty impressive, actually. See, what I did was—"

"Oh, for fuck's sake," Filthy said, looking in my eyes. "You're actually starting to have *fun* with this, aren't you?"

It set me back for a moment.

Fun? No. I wasn't having fun. I was bruised, battered, exhausted, and anxious.

But I had to admit it was kind of exhilarating. Over the years, I'd played a lot of different roles for our burlesque shows—a chef, a priest, a cowboy, a superhero, a starship captain, a teetotaler, a self-help guru, and the president of the United States, to name a few. Hell, I'd even played a detective. But that was on stage, and this was for real. On the run from the cops, the threat of life in prison or worse hanging over my every move, wondering which of the women I was interrogating might suddenly decide to do me in…it was more than enough to get the adrenaline pumping and the heart beating faster.

As was the siren I suddenly heard screaming toward the café. I dropped to the floor and scrambled under the table.

"Again," Filthy said, as the noise passed us and faded into the distance. "Subtle."

"Dropped my, you know, fork." I said, reclaiming my chair.

"Right," she said, mentioning neither that I had risen from the floor with no fork in hand, nor that there had been no fork on the table to begin with. "So after leaving Cherries, you executed a brilliant and no doubt immensely exciting escape from the cops. Skip that part. What did you do next?"

"Called you, came here, and sat on my ass until you arrived."

"Smartest thing you've done in days. And now maybe you'll lay low until this blows over?"

"This isn't blowing over, Filthy. For crying out loud, you had to shake a police escort just to meet me here."

"So instead you're going to—?"

"Take another crack at the other four suspects. Or

rather, five...there's one I haven't talked to at all yet. Hey, you don't happen to know the name of a guy with a beard who wears an overcoat to burlesque shows, do you?"

"Which one?"

"How many do you know?"

"At least one for every show I've ever been in. But come to think of it, I've done my best to make sure I don't know any of their names."

"Fantastic," I said. "Where are you performing to-night?"

"Bottoms Up."

"Do me a favor? Keep an eye out for a guy like that, and if one shows up, send me a message? If you can take a picture of him, that'd be even better."

Filthy sighed. "And what will you be doing?" she asked.

"Hitting as many other shows as I can, to see if I can spot the guy myself."

Filthy took something out of her pocket. She pressed it into my hand. "You might need this," she said. I looked at it. It was a wad of cash. "Just in case," she explained. I took it, but before I could put it in my wallet, Filthy grabbed the back of my head and pulled my face towards hers. She stopped when her lips were the merest fraction of an inch away from mine. I could feel her breath on my chin as she spoke. It was hot, and angry.

"I'm not going to kiss you," she said. "And I'll tell you why not. If you ever want this kiss, the one that you're not getting right now, you're gonna have to do something for it. Do you know what that is?" I shook my head. "You're going to have to get out of this alive. And that means you're going to have to do your damnedest to *keep* yourself alive. Understand?"

She let go of my head, and stood up.

"But—" I said.

"*Alive,*" she said, and left.

CHAPTER 17

I tapped the man in the overcoat on the shoulder.

I'd seen him coming from a block away, headed straight for the Tiki Lodge. With the police looking for me, I figured it was a better idea, instead of actually attending the shows in question, to observe from a safe distance. So I had been lurking in a doorway across the street from the club, wearing an impenetrable disguise: a baseball cap instead of my usual porkpie, with my long, beautiful hair tucked up inside it. Okay, maybe it wasn't exactly impenetrable, but it was enough to make me look different to a casual observer.

So there I was, watching the audience members trickle into the Lodge, when I saw this guy headed in the direction of the venue. Right outfit, right facial hair, right attitude. I ran across the street to intercept the guy and tapped him on the shoulder.

As the man turned around, I realized instantly I had the wrong creep. Other than the superficial qualities of the beard and overcoat, this guy was nothing like the one I had seen at Topkapi. "Sorry," I said. "Thought you were someone I knew."

He walked away, down the block, passing the venue. He wasn't even headed for the show.

This had been my first stop of the night, and it was a bust. Not literally; those were inside the venue. But I had been lurking in that doorway for an hour, and I'd seen neither hide nor hairy beard of my overcoated creep. Now it was 8:30, which meant that the 8:00 show was about to start, and even the latest of late-comers was already inside.

My next stop was Bar Fantastic, to see if my creep liked the bump and grind at the Slap & Tickle Show. He didn't—at least not tonight. There wasn't an over-coat in sight. I moved on.

At the third venue of the night I got a shock. The doorway in which I would have chosen to lurk was already occupied. By a dark figure. A dark and official-looking figure. A dark, official-looking, and Officer Brooklyn-shaped figure.

What was he doing here? I could only imagine that he was waiting for me. He had tracked me down at the Gilded Heel the night before, and now he was waiting for me at another burlesque show. But why this partic-ular show? The sandwich board outside the venue gave me my answer: Jillian, Eva, and Angelina were all per-forming here tonight. Obviously, Officer Brooklyn had pegged this as an event in which I might have a vested interest.

And damn it, it should have been. A show that put so many of my suspects in one room should have been at the top of my list, but I guess the lack of sleep was addling my brain. One of the possible motives I had ascribed to my overcoated creep was that he was an obsessed fan, killing Victoria to get revenge on behalf of one of the performers she had screwed over. If that were the case, the show he was most likely to attend would be a show his favorite performer was in. And with three possible objects of his obsession in one place, the odds were in favor of the creep showing up here.

Well, it didn't matter. I was here now. But with Officer Brooklyn already lurking in my doorway of choice, things got more difficult. There were other hiding places, but where lurked an Officer Brooklyn, there was probably also an Officer Bronx, keeping an eye out in case I tried to do exactly the stupid thing I was currently trying to do.

If I were smart, I'd walk away. Move on to the next show. But three Dreamland performers in one place… it was just too good an opportunity to pass up. So I found another doorway. I stood as far back in it as I could, kept my head tilted down and the brim of my cap in front of my eyes, and hoped that neither Brooklyn nor Bronx would notice me there.

And I watched the crowd.

But my creep didn't show.

Half an hour later, with a final glance towards Officer Brooklyn, I snuck out of my doorway and hightailed it very quietly out of there. I'd risked getting caught for nothing.

The next event, titled simply Raunch, attracted a very specific audience. Overcoat types regularly outnumbered the normal audience. It was like a creep convention was in town for its annual meeting. My particular overcoat might be amongst them, but in order to find out I'd have to look each and every one in the face, and that would be difficult to do without making myself a good deal more obvious than I thought prudent. I gave it a shot—did a quick pass through the crowd waiting on the sidewalk, examining the people as well as I could with the baseball cap pulled down over my eyes—but with no result. My guy might have been there—but if he was, I didn't see him.

The creep search had turned out to be a waste of three hours of my life, hours I couldn't afford. On the other hand, it wasn't like I had alternate plans— the only other thing I could think to do was talk to all the suspects again, to see if they had alibis for the two hours before the show. And since they were currently onstage or waiting to go on, they were un-available.

But maybe I could still salvage the night. After all, they might be performing right now, but after the show, I had a pretty good idea of where they would probably end up…

It's the habit of New York burlesque performers, when finished with their various Saturday gigs, to con-verge on the Daybreak Diner. It's roughly equidistant from several major venues, and the food is neither too greasy nor too expensive. You never know who you'll run into—that's part of the fun—but Jillian regularly stopped in, and I'd seen Eva there few times as well. Angelina was less likely, but given the fact that the three of them were in the same show tonight, and they had plenty to talk about, I thought it was a fairly good bet that she'd tag along this time. If Brioche was working tonight, she'd probably head over as well. And Brioche usually worked on Saturdays.

And it occurred to me that I could kill two birds with one stone. In addition to checking their alibis, I could ask about the creep—maybe one of them had seen him on Wednesday and could identify him.

I headed over, hoping to beat them there. If Officer Brooklyn saw three of his suspects—no matter how little he seemed to suspect them—heading out of the venue together, he would have to follow them as a matter of course.

I scoped out the Daybreak from across the street before I walked in. Thanks to the floor-to-ceiling plate window that served as the street-side wall of the diner, I had a clear view of everyone inside, and there wasn't a performer in sight. So far, so good.

The bell jangled as I opened the door. I kept my head down, hoping the late-night staff wouldn't recognize me in the disguise, though they had recognized me in more improbable getups than this. The fewer people knew I was there, the smaller the likelihood of my cover getting blown. I looked around the room for a quiet spot hide myself while I waited. The booths were no good, and neither were the tables, because as I'd just seen a few moments ago, anyone standing outside could see anyone sitting inside through that window.

I could sit with my back to it, but that meant everyone inside the diner would see me.

Which left only one option. It was somewhat unsavory, but I doubted that even the most diligent police officer would follow a woman into the bathroom. I'd be out of the way of the windows, and come to think of it, it wasn't a bad place to wait for my suspects—chances were that each of them would need to use the facilities at some point.

I sauntered not at all sneakily to the back of the diner. I took a quick glance around to make sure no one was watching me, then walked into the ladies room quickly but confidently. If anyone was inside, I'd apologize profusely, claim confusion, skedaddle, and try again when I saw her leave.

The restroom was empty.

Excellent. But a man standing in the middle of the ladies room would definitely arouse suspicion, if not harassment charges, so I needed a place to hide.

I took the "Employees Must Wash Hands" sign off the mirror and carefully peeled off the tape that had been holding it up. I scribbled "OUT OF ORDER" on the back of the sign, and taped it to the door of one of the stalls. The reused tape was slightly precarious, but it would hold.

That brilliant diversion in place, I ducked inside the stall, locked the door, and put my eye to the crack. Through it, I could see who was walking into the bathroom. If it was someone I wanted to talk to, I would emerge. If it wasn't, I'd hop up on the toilet seat so my feet couldn't be seen under the stall door and keep as quiet as I possibly could while the visitor powdered her nose.

So there I was, at one in the morning, squatting on

the toilet in a stall of the ladies room at the Daybreak Diner. However exhilarating my life was these days, it had certainly become less glamorous.

Ten minutes later, I figured out the major flaw in my strategy: it wasn't one. Squatting on a toilet and hoping the right people would just happen to walk in couldn't be described, even in the loosest terms, as "a plan." I was going to need assistance.

I took out my phone and sent a text message.

And I waited.

Twenty minutes later, in she walked.

"*Need help, meet me in Daybreak ladies room,*" Filthy said as she entered the bathroom, reading from her phone. "You, my darling, are a hopeless romantic."

I told Filthy what I needed.

She grinned. "You want me to figure out how to get four women into this bathroom with you?"

"One at a time," I said.

"Well, that's not as much fun. What should I do, force-feed them water?"

"You're a resourceful gal. You'll figure something out."

"And you'll be alone in the room with each of the possible murderers? Didn't we discuss this?"

"You'll be right outside. If anything happens, I'll scream like a girl and you can come running."

"When this is all over, remind me to bring you back to Jillian's dungeon and leave you there."

"Now who's the hopeless romantic?"

"I'll see what I can do," Filthy said, and left.

I resumed my perch on the toilet and waited.

The door creaked and swung open. Through the gap in the stall door, I saw Jillian walk into the bathroom.

"Hi, Jillian," I said, stepping out into the open.

"Fancy meeting you here," she said.

"You don't seem surprised."

"Filthy told me there was something in the ladies room I might find amusing. I figured it was you."

"Glad you find me amusing."

"Well, I've seen you naked. Mind if I pee?"

"Be my guest. Mind if I ask you a few questions?"

"Shoot," she said, and stepped into one of the stalls.

"You know the creepy guy who was at the Dreamland show?"

"Creepy guys? I know 'em all. I didn't notice one in particular on Wednesday, though. Describe him."

"Wore an overcoat. Had a beard. Sunglasses. A little bit shorter than me."

"That's it?"

"Yeah."

"I can name ten guys who fit that description. They're probably all over at Raunch right now."

"More like twenty. And you have no idea which of them was at Topkapi that night?"

"Sorry, Jonny, I just didn't see him." She stepped out of the stall and went to the sink to wash her hands. "Is that all you wanted to know?"

"About him," I said. "Let's talk about you."

"One of my favorite subjects."

"What were you doing before you came to Topkapi on Wednesday?"

"Why? Never mind, I can guess why. I was teaching a class. My fan dance workshop."

"With students?"

"That's why they call it a class."

"They can verify that?"

"Every one of them. Want a list of their names?"

"When did the class start?"

"At 7:30, but I was meeting with a couple of the students for at least a half hour before that. And before you ask, the class normally ends at 9:30. I wrapped a bit early so I wouldn't be late for the show."

"So when you left the class, you went straight to Topkapi?"

"Dragged my suitcase door to door. You saw me arrive."

"And the walk took you how long?"

"Ten minutes."

"How do I know you didn't take a cab?"

"Because I got there on time," Jillian said. "You know what the traffic is like in that neighborhood at that time of night. It would have taken me twice as long by cab."

"And your students will confirm that you were in that class from 7:30 to 9:30?"

"Why wouldn't they? It's the truth."

It probably was. I would verify it later, but let's face it: if you're going to lie about where you were, you don't involve an entire class full of students. If she had tried to use an S&M client as an alibi, I would have been suspicious; I already knew she could get those guys to do anything she wanted.

Jillian wished me luck, dried her hands on her dress, and left.

I went back into my stall.

The next one in was Eva. When I stepped out of the stall, she laughed and said: "Porky, baby, if I'd known *this* is the sort of thing you were into, I'd have given you a very different kind of lap dance."

"I'm only here to ask you a few questions."

"*Sure* you are." She stepped closer to me and started swaying her hips back and forth.

"Eva, I'm serious. Stop that. I'm still a murder suspect, for crying out loud."

"I know," Eva said, "that's what makes it sooooo sexy. Did he or didn't he? Will he or won't he? Is he going to stick something sharp in me?"

"Right. Anyway. I was wondering—" I shut up because the bathroom door was opening again. "Crap. Quick, into the stall."

"Don't be silly," Eva said. She slammed me against the wall and in one smooth motion unbuttoned and unzipped my pants, pulled them down, shoved her tongue into my mouth, hiked up her skirt to her waist, and began to grind against me.

The woman who walked in was a stranger, thankfully, and seemed flustered to discover a pair of folks en flagrante in el baño. "Oh, uh, sorry," she said, "I didn't, um…" Out of the corner of my eye, I saw her looking at the stalls, as if considering whether to make use of them anyway, but Eva cleared her throat demonstratively, and the visitor lost her nerve and scurried out. As soon as the door was closed, Eva pulled away and lowered her skirt.

"See?" she said. "No problem."

"You're the best murder suspect ever," I observed, pulling up my pants.

"Aw, that's sweet," she said. "So, what did you want to ask me?"

"Do you know the name of the creep in the over-coat who was at the show on Wednesday?"

"What creep?"

"In the front row? He was also standing right by the curtain before the show. Tried to push his way in when we went backstage"

Eva shook her head. "Sorry, Porky," she said. "I wasn't there when the rest of you headed back—I was in the bathroom, remember? Just like right now."

"You don't remember seeing him earlier, though?"

"Honestly, I don't pay a lot of attention to guys like that at shows. I see enough of them at my other job."

"Gotcha," I said. "Okay, then, on a completely different topic: In the two hours or so before you arrived at Topkapi, what were you doing?"

Eva smiled, licked her lips. "Now you're getting personal."

"I am?"

"In this case. Because what I was doing was…" She leaned close and whispered it in my ear.

"Ah," I said. "For the whole two hours?"

Eva shrugged.

"That's quite a long time to be doing that."

Eva shrugged again.

"So you don't have an alibi for those two hours."

"What do you mean?"

"If you were doing what you said you were doing, it's pretty much by definition a solitary activity. For something to count as an alibi, you need to have people who can back it up."

"Oh, I do. Witnesses."

"Witnesses?"

"Sure—the cameraman, the lighting girl, the sound woman, the director, the—"

"Ah," I said.

"I'll give Filthy a copy of the DVD when it comes out. For your birthday."

"That's very sweet," I said, crossing Eva off my mental list. "Thanks."

"That's it? I'm free to go?"

"That's it," I said.

Eva headed toward the door.

"Wait," I called after her. "Don't you need to use the facilities?"

Eva chuckled. "No, Porky. I just came in because Filthy told me you were here. I can't wait to tell her what we did," she said, and left.

I went back into my stall. This had to be the most ignominious series of interrogations ever conducted in the history of murder investigations.

When Brioche came into the bathroom a moment later, I didn't bother to ask her about the creep—I'd gotten as much out of her on that subject as I suspected I ever would. So I went right to the question of what she'd been doing before the show. She offered the oldest answer in the book and the weakest I'd heard yet.

"I was washing my hair," she said.

"Your hair," I said.

"Yes, Jonny Porkpie. My hair. In what way is the statement confusing?"

"Were any of your roommates home? Can they verify that you spent two hours washing your hair?"

"Oh, I wasn't in my house. The hair-washing is a ritualistic statement about the fallacies of the industrial beauty myth as contextualized in contemporary American civilization. I am performing it as an installation piece every night this month at the Miskin Gallery. It's entitled 'Uncleansed Locks: The Sham of Shampoo.' I walk through the crowd, completely naked, and seat myself in a bathtub in the center of the gallery, which represents the internal conflict between representation and essence—"

I'll skip the rest. I didn't need to hear it and neither do you. What it boiled down to was that Brioche, too, had a roomful of people who could verify her whereabouts from six o'clock until ten minutes before she arrived at Topkapi.

One more woman out of the running.

That left only one. The one I'd suspected it might come down to: the victim's own most recent victim, Angelina.

✿

About ten minutes later, she walked in. She was back in character—or rather, back out of character. I was pretty sure that the Angelina of burlesque was closer to her real personality than the one I'd seen in the offices of the trade magazine fulfillment services company. The thick black eyeliner was back on, the long black hair was down again, and the outfit was black and gothic again.

This interview was going to be trickier than the others, both because Angelina was now my number one suspect and because she was the least positively disposed toward me of all the women in the show. If any of these women were likely go running to the cops to get me arrested, it was her. I decided that the best plan was to put myself between Angelina and the exit before she realized who I was.

I was almost quick enough. But I guess something about the way I was moving made her suspicious, or maybe it was the fact that I'd stepped out of a stall with an "OUT OF ORDER" sign on the door. She stuck a foot out as I was attempting to sneak by. I tripped on it and fell face down on the tile floor.

I rolled over quickly, but not quickly enough to avoid the knee that pressed itself to my throat. I felt her fishnets against my neck.

"Hi," I squeaked.

"You," she said.

"Yeah. Hey, could you…?" I said, tapping on her leg. She shook her head, but eased up enough that I could breathe again.

"What the hell are you doing in here?" she said.

"I want to ask you a couple more questions, Angelina. Then I'll leave you alone."

She snorted. "I suppose it's easier on my girlfriend's knuckles then having her beat the crap out of you again." She swung her knee off my throat and I pulled myself up. "You have lipstick all over your face," she said.

I wiped my mouth on the back of my arm.

Angelina crossed her arms and waited for me to talk.

"There was a guy in an overcoat at the show on Wednesday—do you know who he was?" I said.

"No."

"Did you see him?"

"No."

"He was hanging out by the curtain."

"Didn't see him."

"How long were you at Topkapi before I arrived?"

"Didn't see you come in."

"Before Cherries arrived, then."

"I don't know, five minutes. However long it takes to stash a bag, order a drink, and sit down."

"First time you were at the venue that day?"

"Yes."

"Where did you come from?"

"Dinner."

"Where?"

"Midtown. Near my office. Krash met me after work."

"When's that?"

"I get out at 6:30."

"Can the people at the restaurant verify that you were there?"

"I have the credit card receipt. You want to see that? Shall I show you that?" She dug in her purse, pulled out a black leather wallet, rifled through it, snatched out a slip of paper and shoved it in my face. "There. Happy?"

I looked at the date on the receipt—this past Wednesday—and the time. Then I looked at the address of the restaurant.

"How did you get downtown?" I asked. Instead of answering, she shoved another receipt at me. This one was for a taxi. A taxi that had dropped her off at Topkapi at exactly the time she claimed to have arrived.

"Are we done?" said Angelina.

"Soon. Look, tell me this: Why did you insist on doing the show that night?"

"I'd been booked for months."

"But LuLu asked you to switch dates. Why wouldn't you do it?"

"LuLu never asked me to switch dates. I wouldn't have done it even if she had—I'm not inclined to do that woman any favors—but she didn't."

"What do you mean you're—?"

"Enough," she said, pushing me out of the way. "You said a couple questions, that was over a dozen. I'll use the men's room."

The door creaked shut behind her.

✽

Would she call the cops? All I could do was hope not. I couldn't do anything to prevent it, since I was stuck in this bathroom until I knew for a fact there were no longer any cops watching the Daybreak.

I washed my face in the sink and reclaimed my perch in the stall. My theory was, rather appropriately for my surroundings, down the toilet, so I needed to come up with a new hypothesis, and quick. There was still the creep in the overcoat, but nobody who might have seen him had any idea who he was, and if I hadn't been able to track him down on a Saturday night packed with shows, I wasn't optimistic about my chances of finding him at all. And if all I had to work with was my original five suspects, I was going to need to come up with a version of events that didn't require the murderer to have seen Victoria walking into the venue at the time she stowed her bag. Who was the philosopher who claimed he did his best thinking on the can? Archimedes? Or was that in the bathtub? At any rate, it wasn't working for me. When the door opened again a few minutes later, the only thing that had come up was a cramp in my leg.

"You still in here?" Filthy's voice echoed off the tile walls.

"Where would I go?" I kicked open the stall door. "Step into my office."

"You get what you needed?"

"Not really."

"That's not what Eva said."

"Filthy—"

"Nice girl. We should really have her over for dinner sometime."

As enjoyable as the suggestion sounded, I just wasn't in the mood right now. "Everybody had alibis," I explained, pacing back and forth across the bathroom. "All of them. Still need to be verified, but I've got a feeling they'll all check out. They seem pretty damn solid." I stopped in front of Filthy and looked her in the eyes. "Unless you're lying about that dinner, Filthy, and Cherries did it. With you. You and Cherries. Together."

"Wow," she said. "You're really that desperate?"

"Pretty much," I said. "All I've accomplished tonight is to investigate myself right back into being the main suspect. Oh, except for a creepy guy no one but me and Brioche seems to remember."

What she didn't say was *I told you so*. I could tell that she wanted to, but she didn't. It's one of the reasons our marriage has lasted as long as it has. Instead, she said: "Buy you a drink, sailor?"

"Buy me a bottle."

She shoved me back into my stall. "I'll come get you when the coast is clear," she said, and left the bathroom. I closed the door and reclaimed my perch.

A couple minutes passed, but Filthy didn't come back.

Five minutes.

Ten minutes.

Fifteen.

It made sense. People tended to linger after they

ate. She was just waiting for people to clear out before she came back for me. The delay didn't mean anything, I told myself. It didn't mean anything at all.

Twenty minutes.

Twenty-five.

Finally, I heard the creak of hinges. I pulled my legs up, just in case it wasn't Filthy coming back, and peeked through the crack.

The bathroom door was opening slowly, slowly. That was weird.

And no one was walking in. That was weird, too.

Then I saw the movement—it was hard to make out with the limited visibility the gap in the stall allowed, but I thought I could see a hand coming through the door. It was reaching into the bathroom, feeling around on the wall.

Why?

The light switch. The hand was looking for the light switch.

And it found it, and flipped it.

Blackout.

Usually, to a guy like me, a blackout signals the beginning of a show…or the end. I was hoping this particular blackout wasn't indicating the latter.

The door swung open. A figure was briefly silhouetted against the light of the diner behind. It wasn't a woman's figure.

The door groaned closed, leaving the room completely dark.

A faucet was dripping, across the room. I hadn't noticed it before. In the dark, it echoed eerily. Ominously. It was dripping ominously.

Drip. Drip.

The echo was louder than the footsteps were.

Drip.

The footsteps were very quiet.

Drip, drip.

And they were making their way toward my stall. Creeping in my direction. Very very slowly.

The air conditioning fan kicked in. It hummed, a throbbing rusty whir, not quite drowning out the dripping. But drowning out those footsteps.

I'd felt better when I could hear them.

Whuh whuh whuh. The AC fan, overhead. *Drip.* The faucet. Outside the bathroom, the muffled sounds of a diner doing normal business. Silverwear on dishes. Plates clattering. The low hum of conversation.

Hours passed.

Seconds passed.

Days passed.

No time passed at all.

Whuh whuh whuh whuh.

Drip drip, drip drip.

Tap, tap, tap.

That last sound—the tapping—was on my stall door. A light but insistent knocking. I held my breath.

The knocking kept going. And I could hear the breathing of the person doing it. The breathing of someone either overweight or perhaps wearing a heavy overcoat in the middle of summer. A sinister breathing. An evil breathing.

Another knock.

I stayed where I was.

Drip…drip…thump—CRASH!

Hardware ripped from the frame as the door swung in at me. I jumped back, hitting my spine on the pipes behind. The door banged against the wall. The figure stepped towards me, and I heard a—

Click.

CHAPTER 18

The dark was less blinding than the light.

The flashlight was directly in my eyes. I put a hand up to block my face, but the spots still swam in my retinas. The light traveled down my body, rested for a moment on the toilet, and then crept slowly back up to my face.

I heard a chuckle. A triumphant chuckle.

I was going to die on this toilet.

CHAPTER 19

"Am I interrupting something?"

The voice of Officer Brooklyn was large enough to fill the entire ladies room of the Daybreak Diner.

" 'Cause if I'm interrupting somethin'," he said, putting the flashlight under his arm as he reached for the pair of handcuffs on his belt, "I can always come back later."

CHAPTER 20
SUNDAY

"So lemme get this straight, *Senator*," Officer Brooklyn said, leaning back in his chair. I had already reminded him several times that my title of choice was "the Burlesque Mayor of New York City," but he had decided he preferred "Senator of Striptease," and he wasn't the type to let things go. "You were tryin' to track down some creepy guy in an overcoat with scraggly hair, a scraggly beard, and sunglasses. A guy who just happened to be at the show that night, and who you claim is the only person who could possibly be the murderer."

The interrogation room of the Ninth Precinct was every bit as charming as it had been when I was last here, though the intervening days had left it a bit dingier. But then, so was I. I'd never been invited to a slumber party in a New York City precinct house before, and hoped never to be again. Officers Brooklyn and Bronx had taken me out of the cell in the early hours of the morning and shoved me back into this room with a stale donut and a surprisingly good cup of coffee. The case file was spread out on the table in front of me, with a photo of Victoria's corpse on the top of the pile of papers, where, I imagined, they hoped it would tweak my conscience. The two detectives had

taken turns trying to convince me that I was a murderer. Brooklyn was currently at bat.

"That's right," I replied.

Brooklyn shook his head. "That's a pretty flimsy
premise. For a creative guy, you ain't too creative."

"This guy spent more time near Victoria's bag than
anyone else. Nobody else had the opportunity to plant
that poison."

"Well, sure. If he's real. But you know, the laws of
the City of New York are pretty clear on the fact that I
can't arrest a guy you made up. Why did you say this
mysterious pervert wanted to kill the girl, again?"

I hadn't said, because—given that I hadn't actually
managed to track the creep down—I had no idea. The
truth was, I knew no more about him than Officer
Brooklyn did...well, maybe slightly more, because I
knew that he existed, and Brioche would back me up
on that point. But I had a feeling that she wouldn't
make a very credible witness.

Brooklyn leaned over the table and looked me in
the eye. "Senator, I'm gonna give it to you straight.
You're in a bad way. I'll tell you what we got on you,
and then you can decide whether you want to make it
easy on yourself. There's the motive, check. There's
the fingerprints on the bottle, check. There's the fifty
witnesses who saw you hand it to her. There's all the
harassment of the other women in the show, doesn't
look good. There's that convenience store you stopped
into on Friday. You buy a bottle of the exact same
poison that killed the girl—the only bottle of that
poison in that store, and you toss it in the trash right

outside. Why? I don't know. But it don't look good. And then the kicker, Senator, the kicker is you ducking out on us Friday night. Oh, yeah—your bartender friend told us you were in there. That just screams guilty. In large, capital letters."

He tapped the table with his finger.

"So I'm gonna tell you again, Senator, what I told you the first time you were down here: give it up, and it will go easier on you."

"Have you ruled out suicide?" I asked.

"Oh, come on, Senator."

"No, really," I said. "What if Victoria found out she was being set up to be humiliated. She finally realized her career in burlesque was over. Too many people knew what she'd done. So maybe she decides to go out with a bang, take revenge on the people who she blames for her situation, by making us all suspects in her murder. She buys the poison, gets me to hand it to her, drinks it, and dies with a smile on her face, knowing she was putting all of us in hot water."

"Does that look like a smile on her face?" Officer Brooklyn asked, pushing the photo of Victoria's corpse towards me. It didn't.

"The smile isn't the point. The point is—"

"Hey, here's one," Officer Brooklyn suggested, "I don't believe you didn't think of this. Maybe alligators crawled up from the sewer and put the poison in that bag. But they didn't stay for the show because they went off to sell someone the Brooklyn Bridge."

"Okay, then," I offered, "What about the accident angle? That she packed the wrong bottle by mistake?"

"Oh, yeah. That might hold some water, but only if we hadn't already searched the apartment she was staying in, from top to bottom. Not a single bottle to be found, real or fake. Any other crackpot theories, or are you ready to confess?"

"Listen," I said. "Whoever switched Victoria's fake poison for real poison had to know in advance that she was going to do Angelina's poison number. I didn't. I'd never even seen Angelina do it, never mind Victoria. Hell, I didn't even know Victoria was going to be in the show that night until two seconds before she walked in the room. Don't you think that makes it a little difficult for me to be the killer?"

Brooklyn shrugged.

"Nice try, Senator, but truth is, it don't matter how you found out Angelina was doing the number—"

"Victoria."

"What?"

"You meant to say, 'how you found out Victoria was doing the number.' Victoria, not Angelina. Angelina is the one Victoria stole the number from. Victoria is the one who…" My voice trailed off. Something had just clicked into place in my head, like a bra being fastened.

"Angelina, Victoria, Titsy McGee, don't matter. You know who I meant," said Officer Brooklyn. "The dead girl. I don't know how you knew she was doing the number that night, and frankly it don't matter one little bit. It ain't gonna make or break my case. You found out, you brought the poison with you to the show, you killed her in front of fifty witnesses. Now why don't you—"

"Hold it," I said.

"Excuse me? Hold it? You want me to hold it?" He pushed his chair back and stood up. "Oh, I'll hold it all right."

"No, I mean—" What I meant was that Brooklyn's slip of the tongue had finally made the whole thing come together. "What would you say to one more crackpot theory, Officer?"

Brooklyn's eyes narrowed. He sat down again.

"Make it good, Senator," he said. "Make it good."

"It will be," I said. "And you'll want to listen closely. Because if I'm right, the murderer is going to strike again, and soon."

He snorted.

But a minute later, he leaned forward and started taking notes.

CHAPTER 21

So, there I was, lying on the stage, straddled by a beautiful and completely naked woman. I rocked back and forth with her as she bounced on top of me, our bodies locked together, thrusting, thrusting. A sound was coming from the back of her throat—something between a moan and a growl. Me? I was grunting with each thrust, too, but couldn't manage much more in terms of vocalization, because one of her hands was pressed firmly to my mouth.

It's *exactly* as exciting as it sounds.

But not in the way you think.

Music started.

The curtains peeled back, revealing us to the audience. A packed house.

When they saw us, they began to cheer. And hoot. And holler. And whistle.

Great way to open a show.

If only I hadn't been fighting for my life.

The naked woman, of course, was Victoria's murderer.

The thing she was thrusting was a knife.

Twenty minutes earlier, that same naked woman was looking at me in the dressing room mirror at the Gilded Heel.

I stood on the stage, right outside the door of the dressing room. It was just the two of us. The other performers hadn't arrived yet. The murderer was getting herself ready for the pre-show go-go set. According to the Gilded Heel's website, she wasn't scheduled to perform that night. Yet here she was, as I suspected she would be. How did I know? Because I knew the identity of her next victim, and that next victim *was* scheduled to perform. My murderer had no doubt traded bookings with another performer to be here.

Which meant that, some time later in the evening, if things went as she planned, a homicidal ecdysiast would be in this cramped little dressing room with her intended victim.

I'd worked out my entrance line on the way over—the first thing I'd say when I saw her.

I had just said it: "You set me up."

She stiffened when she heard my voice.

"Didn't they arrest you?" she said.

"They let me go when I told them who the real murderer was."

"Let me guess, Porkpie…I'm supposed to say 'Oh, who's that?' and then you, in a voice rich with drama and pity, reply 'You.'"

Sadly, that was exactly what I'd planned. I guess when you open with '*You set me up*,' the rest of the conversation is fairly predictable.

"Very dramatic, Porkpie," she said. "Unfortunately, you have no idea what you're talking about."

"I wish that were true," I said.

She turned to face me.

I was treated to the last full-frontal view of LuLu LaRue that I would ever enjoy.

I adjusted the brim of my porkpie.

"But you're the one who killed her, LuLu. And I'll be damned if I'm going to jail for it."

The DJ popped his head through the curtains. "Ready to go-go in five minutes?" he asked.

LuLu nodded her head, curtly, and he retreated.

"You're not going to be ready to go-go in five minutes," I told her. "You might be available in twenty-five to life. But I doubt anyone's going to want to watch you then."

"You're a real piece of work, Porkpie, you know that? Accusing me of murder to try to cover your own ass. And here I thought we were friends. It's ludicrous. I was *out of town*, or did you forget? That's the whole reason you were running my show in the first place."

I shook my head. "Here's the problem I had," I began.

"Oh, that's it? That's all? You're not even going to acknowledge the fact that there's no possible way I could be the murderer?"

"I'm not," I said, "because you are. Here was my problem: the murder weapon. A prop in an act. In order to plan a murder using a performer's own prop, you have to know in advance that she's going to be using the prop on the night you're planning to kill her. In this case, no one did. No one knew Victoria was doing that act; except for you and Cherries, no one even knew she was in the show."

LuLu chuckled. "Look at you, Porkpie. Standing onstage, doing the grand finale. It's like your murder mystery show—you've got the killer cornered, or you think you do, and you're all ready for the big reveal. It's cute, Porkpie—but if 'no one' knew she was doing that act, that includes me."

"True," I said. "But I realized something as I was talking to the cops: The murderer didn't have to know *Victoria* was doing that act. She just had to know that *someone* was doing that act."

"Someone," she said. "Some mysterious act-doing person."

"Three people knew that act was going to be performed that night. Angelina knew Angelina was doing the original version. Victoria knew Victoria was doing the plagiarized version. And you knew...not about Victoria, but about Angelina. You knew the odds were excellent Angelina was going to do that act. Because you set her up to do it *by telling her not to.*"

"Wow," said LuLu. "Reverse psychology. What a devious criminal mind I have."

"Look, Angelina and I aren't exactly close, but even I know her well enough to guess how she'd react if someone told her she could do any act but one. And, sure enough, that's how she reacted. She brought the number you told her not to."

"So?"

"So when you got to Topkapi on Wednesday night—"

"We're forgetting, then, that I was out of town? I still have my train ticket, punched by the conductor and everything."

"I'm sure you do. You're not stupid. Which is why you know that's no alibi at all. There are a thousand ways you could have returned to the city for the show. And as soon as the police start digging, they'll find how you did it, even if you were smart enough to make the trip wearing the disguise you had on when you showed up at Topkapi. Keeping them strapped down for all that time must have been pretty hard on the boobs, huh?"

LuLu started. She had unconsciously been massaging a breast. She looked at me, and for the first time I saw a crack in the façade. I went on.

"You put on an overcoat to hide your hips, glued on a beard to cover your face, added a wig to conceal whatever the beard didn't and a pair of sunglasses to hide your eyes. Not even the people who have seen you perform in Allan Schmuck drag would recognize you in that get-up. And the final touch: the character himself, the sort of guy no one wants to examine too closely. You know from personal experience that most performers will go out of their way to avoid eye contact with a creep like that.

"You fooled me, that's for sure. Even when you tried to force your way in early—risky, but a nice touch. It really sold the character. I didn't suspect for a minute. Neither did Brioche, and she *talked* to you—that must have been a tense few minutes, but you pulled it off. You're good, LuLu. Always have been."

"Gee, thanks," she said. Her voice was tight. "Coming from a man trying to set me up for murder, that's a real compliment."

"So," I said, "you show up at Topkapi in full creep drag. No risk there—if anyone does recognize you, you just tell them you're there undercover to see how the show runs when you're gone, or some such nonsense. When you arrive, you look around to make sure Angelina is there, and you see her canoodling with her blue-mohawked girlfriend."

I watched LuLu carefully as I said this. She kept her face completely still, but there was a slight, involuntary twitch of her eye.

"You wait until I stash Cherries' bag for her, and then you duck behind the curtain when no one is looking. There are four black drag-bags in the alcove, all of them more or less identical. No problem, you think, the contents will tell me which one I'm after. And that was your big mistake. Because there was no way you could have known—no way anyone could have known—that two of these nearly identical bags would also have nearly identical contents. You open them one by one until you find the prop bottle you're looking for, and then you replace it with the real poison and slip back out to mingle with the crowd at the bar. How could you possibly know that you'd tampered with the wrong bag?

"The suitcase you opened first was Victoria's," I said. "But the person you were trying to kill was Angelina."

LuLu smiled. It wasn't a friendly smile.

"Your first inkling that something might be wrong comes when Victoria's walks onto the stage. There you are, sitting in the front row, waiting to observe the results of your handiwork, and all of a sudden someone else is doing the act you expected Angelina to do, with a prop identical to the one you sabotaged. Or is it in fact the very one you sabotaged? It's a fifty-fifty chance. Maybe you were tempted to stop the act before it went too far—but you couldn't, not without revealing what you'd done. So instead you just sat there. Sat there and waited to see what would happen…

"And what happened, happened."

LuLu's face was still expressionless, but there was something in her eyes. Something I'd never seen there before.

"So there it is. There's really only two questions left. The first, of course, is why you were trying to kill Angelina. I think I've got that one figured out. The way you talk about her, the way she talks about you, the way you reacted a couple minutes ago when I mentioned her canoodling with her new girlfriend—the whole thing reeks of bad breakup."

LuLu said nothing, but she pursed her lips.

"But the second question completely baffles me," I said, turning to block the dressing room doorway. "If your real objective was to kill Angelina, why did you go to all the trouble of setting up the whole elaborate 'Just Desserts' show?"

She didn't try to run, or do any of the other things you might expect a murderer to do when caught—panic, confess, break down in tears. Instead, she looked me straight in the eye, lifted a finger to her mouth, and ran her tongue along the length of it.

"Porkpie, Porkpie, Porkpie," she said. "You're a performer, sweetheart, I'd think the answer to that question would be obvious." She brought the hand down. I tried to keep my eyes on her face, but couldn't help noticing that she was making small circles on her breast with the wet fingertip.

"I guess it isn't," I said. "I don't suppose you'd like to tell me?"

She pinched her nipple. Something in her eyes changed as it stiffened. Her smile widened.

"Misdirection," she said. And that was when she jumped me with the knife.

We tumbled backwards through the door of the dressing room and out onto the stage.

When the curtains opened, the audience cheered and hollered—I'm sure it looked great, but this was no performance. I was barely managing to keep myself alive. LuLu isn't a weak woman, and since she was on top, she had gravity on her side.

The knife plunged towards me, aimed at my chest. I smacked at her wrist, hoping to deflect the blow. I did, but not enough. Something very sharp slipped into my shoulder.

Ow.

LuLu yanked the blade out of my arm and raised it over her head to try again. I grabbed her wrist.

The stage lights flashed in time with the music. Red. Green. Blue. The vicious grimace on LuLu's face was especially disturbing in the green. I don't know why they even have green lights at burlesque venues —that color doesn't make anyone look good.

I held her arm away from me with every bit of strength I had.

LuLu thrashed back and forth, trying to twist out of my grip. I felt a drop of something hit my forehead. As the light changed from red to blue, I could see there was blood dripping down my arm where the knife had sliced my wrist.

Ow, again.

LuLu felt me weakening, and grinned. I looked into her eyes, and saw nothing of the woman who was once my friend. She wrenched her hand away from mine and raised the knife again for one last fatal plunge.

The ones who saved my life were, of all people, Officers Brooklyn and Bronx.

You didn't think that they were going to let me leave that station house all by myself, did you?

No matter how convincing my story was, no matter how urgent the theoretical need to prevent a second murder, I was still their main suspect.

The disco ball on the ceiling of the Gilded Heel threw tiny sparkles over the two detectives as they came barreling through the crowd like two very short trucks, knocking over glasses, bottles, and a bachelorette or two. They were yelling something. I couldn't hear it.

But for the first time since we'd met, I was glad to see them.

The cops jumped onto the stage just as LuLu was about to carve herself a tasty slice of Porkpie. Bronx grabbed LuLu's arm in mid-stab and twisted until she dropped the weapon. Brooklyn took her other arm and together they stood her up.

"He was trying to kill me," LuLu yelled. "He was trying to kill me!"

Bronx took a set of handcuffs from her belt and locked them around LuLu's wrists.

As the queen of Dreamland Burlesque stood on the stage for the last time, the lights flashed green, red, blue over her naked body.

The sirens of the cop cars pulling up outside weren't loud enough to drown out the music.

The DJ reached for the rope to close the curtains.

The crowd loved it. LuLu's final performance got a standing ovation.

CHAPTER 22

"So," I said. "As requested, I didn't get myself killed."

"Barely," Filthy said.

"And I stayed out of jail, too. A kiss, I believe, was promised?"

"Gosh, I'd love to," said Filthy. "But now that your lurid tale of death and revenge is over, I should remind you that we're supposed to be debuting a new number in two days, and because you've been gallivanting about with all your sexy murder suspect pals, we haven't rehearsed it once."

"Ah, but the story's not over yet," I replied. "Of course, if you think rehearsing is more important than a few more minutes of my exciting adventures…" I sighed, and stood up.

"Okay, fine." She pushed me back down onto the couch. "Have your fun. I guess you've earned it. The cops saved your ass, and then what happened?"

"No kiss?"

"Like you said, story's not over yet. I don't know how it ends. Maybe you don't survive."

"Cute," I said. "Officer Bronx led me and LuLu out of the Gilded Heel, which, as you know, isn't easy when the place is packed. At the door, we ran into Angelina and Krash, who had arrived just in time to see my brave, valiant and entirely sexy life-and-death struggle…"

○

Officer Brooklyn asked Angelina to join us on the trip to the Ninth Precinct. Angelina turned him down with her usual grace and poise, which is to say, not very much. But when he explained that he needed her, as the intended murder victim, to make a statement about her relationship with LuLu, she changed her tune pretty damn quick.

"Intended murder victim?" Angelina said, her voice cracking. Krash grabbed her elbow. Officer Brooklyn brought them up to date on the situation, making a particular point (and very nice of him, too) of the fact that by coming here tonight, I had probably saved Angelina from a second attempt on her life.

Angelina looked at me. Then, all of a sudden, she wrapped her arms around me and squeezed. Never in a million years (and especially in the last few days) would I have expected to be on the receiving end of an affectionate hug from Angelina Blood. She and I have been good pals ever since, by the way. Some of the best friendships start with a healthy dose of antagonism, I suppose. (Oh, and Krash's band isn't all that bad either, for heavy metal. But if you go see them play, bring earplugs.)

Krash thanked me too, in her own way. "You're all right," she said, and gave me a friendly punch in the arm. The one in which I'd just been stabbed. Ow.

At the station, Officer Bronx put LuLu behind bars —they had her, if nothing else, on the attempted murder of yours truly. She was still protesting that she was the victim, that I was trying to frame her for Victoria's murder, but the police weren't buying. They took a statement from Angelina. They also insisted on a full account of my own activities for the past few days, which took longer, because Officer Brooklyn had to stop me periodically to laugh at my detective skills.

"Still, for an amateur…" he didn't finish the sentence. Instead, he stood up and held out his hand. I shook it. "All right, buddy," he said. "You're off the hook. We might have a couple more questions for you, and you'll probably need to testify at some point, but you're a free man."

"That's the nicest thing you've ever said to me, Officer." I donned my hat and made my way to the door.

"Ay, Senator," Officer Brooklyn yelled after me. "Good luck with the strippin', right?"

I pulled a postcard out of my pocket and handed it to him. "Give me a call if you want to come see a show," I said. "It's on me."

"Nah, I couldn't," he said. "Wife would kill me."

"Bring her," I said. "She'll enjoy it, too."

"So here I am, baby," I said. *"The cops are off my tail and that means there's room on it for a knockout like you. You're looking at a mug who was under the rough thumb of John Q. Law and managed to wriggle out using only his porkpie-clad noggin and a pair of rough fists. I looked down the dark tunnel of forever, baby, and I came back alive to collect my smooch—"*

"And LuLu?" Filthy interrupted.

"Well, gee, given the fact that she tried to kill me *and* frame me for murder in the same week, I think I can write off that particular friendship. Plus there's the fact that she's a homicidal maniac who's going to spend the rest of her life in jail. That might get in the way, too."

"Still," Filthy said. "It's too bad. She was a great performer."

"So she'll be a big hit in the prison talent show."

"Ooh, tacky."

"I was thinking, it's kind of ironic. About Victoria, I mean. She was a plagiarist to the end. She even stole someone else's death."

"Tackier still."

"I've been called worse," I said. "Oh, here's another juicy bit of gossip: Officer Brooklyn told me they're shutting down Topkapi. You wouldn't believe the fire and health code violations they found when they searched it. Apparently, the place was a deathtrap."

"So to speak," said Filthy.

"And there we are. That's the end of the story, and I remain miraculously alive. Where, then, is the afore-mentioned kiss?"

"Fine." She gave me a quick peck on the lips. "Now can we rehearse?"

I sighed. "I suppose."

Filthy unbuttoned my pants and unzipped my fly. Then she pulled down her skirt. No underpants, of course.

She left her shirt on, though. A nice red shirt, though not as bright as her hair.

Button-down.

She started the music, and shoved me onto the floor.

"Hey, detective…" she said. "How'd you like to dive into another case?"

Actually, we didn't end up rehearsing at all.